Run *DONNY* Run !

Run DONNY *Run !*

Joe Buckley

First published 1991 by
WOLFHOUND PRESS
68 Mountjoy Square
Dublin 1

Wolfhound Press receives financial assistance from
The Arts Council/An Chomhairle Ealaíon, Dublin, Ireland.

British Library Cataloguing in Publication Data
Buckley, Joe
    Run Donny, run.
    I. Title
    823. 914 [F]

    ISBN 0-86327-297-5

Cover design: Joanne Finegan
Typesetting by Seton Music Graphics Ltd, Bantry, Co Cork
Printed by TechMan Ltd., Dublin.

1

Donny O'Sullivan had torn the corner off another page of his English copy and was slipping it into his mouth, when the teacher's shadow fell on his desk. Donny was happy enough with his homework. He had finished selling his newspapers early last evening, gone home and done it under the weak centre light in his room.

'Ah, no breakfast this morning, Donny?' Bill Moloney, known affectionately to his students as 'Boloney', enquired with gentle sarcasm, noting the ragged corner of the page. Donny couldn't really tell the truth — that he was thinking about the trouble at home and barely noticed his nervous habit of chewing paper.

'No, Sir,' he replied cheerfully. 'Lost the toss for the last cornflake.' Bill, who had bent down to see the homework more clearly, straightened up slowly. Donny didn't look up at him. Instead he looked at Flagon, his mate, who sat beside him. He knew by the grin on Flagon's face that it was OK. Bill Moloney moved on, shaking his head slowly. 'Lost the toss for the last cornflake,' he repeated in his mind. He was savouring this one, keeping it fresh for the staff-room at lunch hour.

When the bell had rung and the boys were shuffling out, Bill called to Donny O'Sullivan. 'Donny, a quick word.' Donny stopped by the teacher's desk, fixing the collar of his denim jacket.

'Everything OK, Donny?' Bill asked as he gathered up his papers. 'I thought you looked a bit down today.' Donny brushed back his black hair with his hand.

'Oh, it's nothing much,' he replied. 'Just a bit of trouble at home. It'll blow over.'

His brown eyes, set in a strong face, looked directly at the teacher, and he spoke in the easy manner of one who, though still only sixteen, was used to dealing with grown-ups on an equal footing.

'I'll be around after school for a while today, if you feel like talking about it,' Bill offered.

'I might do that, Sir,' replied Donny. He shifted slightly towards the door. 'But . . . Eh . . . We've got Jaws, I mean, Brother Sharkey now.'

'Oh, gosh! I'm sorry, Donny,' replied Bill, moving towards the door. 'Carry on. We don't want you to get chewed up again.' He watched Donny's athletic figure as he hurried out. 'If there's any problem, you just refer him to me, you hear?' he called after him.

Donny had had a run-in with Brother Sharkey, the Technical Drawing teacher, only the previous week. He had been late leaving the house that morning because Maeve, his sister, had been having another row with her husband, Liam. Donny had stayed in his room, a knot of anxiety in his stomach, until he'd heard Liam slam his way out of the house. When he had finally reached the school, he had remembered with dismay that he had forgotten to ask his distressed sister for a note explaining his lateness. School rules required such a note and, while other teachers would have accepted his word for it, Brother Sharkey was a stickler for the rules.

Donny had realised later that he had made two tactical errors that morning. He should have waited in the toilets until Brother Sharkey's class was finished, and he shouldn't have let the Brother see the anger in his eyes when he imposed on Donny his customary punishment for lateness without a note — a four-page essay on punctuality. Brother Sharkey's nickname was 'Jaws' and he ruled his classroom with military discipline. He couldn't tolerate any sign of insubordination in his pupils, and so Donny became a marked man. That was why he now hurried out of Bill Moloney's classroom, down the stairs, taking four steps at a time, and ran noiselessly along the corridor towards the Technical Drawing room. He arrived just as the door closed in his face.

'Rats!' he said to himself. He opened the door and went in. Jaws was standing inside the door with his back to Donny. The class was already quiet, each boy busy with his drawing sheets. Donny closed the door and moved around beside the Brother.

'Late again, O'Sullivan!' There was a strange hardness in the voice. Jaws didn't turn to look at him.

'I'm sorry, Brother. I was talking to . . . .'

'Stand over there!' barked the Brother, pointing to a space beside the teacher's desk. Donny didn't move.

'Brother, I was talking to Mr Moloney, and he told me to refer you to him . . . .' Jaws turned to look at him now. His face was expressionless except for a slight quivering of muscles in the jaw. But his eyes were frightening. They gleamed at Donny with a black intensity, in which he could see no feeling, not even anger. The class had gone very quiet now and he knew they were all willing him to go and stand by the teacher's desk, especially Flagon and Swamp, his two best friends. Jaws stared at him for a full five seconds. Donny looked steadily into the black eyes.

'Stand at the desk!' the Brother said again. Donny knew he should go, but something inside him told him it was wrong to give in to this tyranny.

'Why?' he asked instead. What sounded like a whispered groan came from Flagon's direction. Donny saw the flush come into the Brother's neck and the tension into his right arm. He saw the clenched fist coming across but Donny was too fast. He ducked and stepped back between the rows of desks. When Jaws came for him again, he vaulted lightly over Murphy's desk into the next row. He picked up an empty chair and held it in front of him. Flagon, on his left, half rose from his seat.

'No, Flag!' Donny said.

Jaws stood there like a frustrated old bull. He raised a pudgy finger.

'O'Sullivan! You're gone!' he growled hoarsely through his teeth. 'I'm going to get Brother O'Connor! You're finished in this school!' he almost shouted as he rushed out.

The class erupted with restrained elation and dismay. They were proud of him, but afraid for him too.

'Jays, Donny!' breathed Flagon, as the seriousness of the situation dawned on him.

'It's OK, Flag. Don't get involved. I'll see you later.' He went to the window and slid it up. 'Tell Boloney, will you?' he asked them. Then he climbed out onto the path. Ten paces took him to the wall and, in a moment, he was on the street, walking fast. His anger was fading and he felt his knees go rubbery under him. Now he was really in trouble.

2

Maeve, his sister, was lying on the settee in the sitting room when Donny let himself in. She looked at her watch in surprise.

'You're home early?' she said. Donny saw her puffed lips and the discoloured swelling under her right eye. She had been crying.

'Yeah. Got off a bit early,' he lied. 'How are you?' He dropped his bag and came closer. She turned her head away a little. Her brunette hair was dishevelled.

'I'll be OK,' she said, dropping her eyes. An involuntary sob escaped her. Donny felt the hate rising in him.

'I'll kill him if he ever touches you again!'

'No, Donny. Don't say anything to him. It'll only make things worse. It's just that he's under pressure. They're pushing him for the money and he just can't pay it at the moment.'

'That's still no excuse!'

'Well, maybe I shouldn't have called him a waster,' she said.

Donny sat on the arm of the settee, clenching his hands around his knee. He had never spoken directly to Maeve about her marriage. She was the only family he had now. Their mother had died when he was only three. He couldn't remember anything about her, although he had often lain awake at night trying to force a memory from his consciousness. His dad had looked after him and Maeve until the accident four years before. Donny remembered him as a soft-spoken man, a good man. He had left the house to Maeve and Donny, and nearly eight thousand pounds each in trust until they were twenty-one.

Within a year of their dad's death, Maeve had become engaged. Donny had never liked Liam, with his fancy overcoats and flash second-hand cars and his talk of big business deals. With dismay Donny had watched Maeve, still only nineteen, being dazzled by the social swirl and the fast talk. Sensing his opposition, Maeve would cajole and persuade and bribe him into being civil when Liam came to visit. After the wedding, Liam moved in 'temporarily like' until he had 'organised the few bob for the house above in Templeogue'. But that was three years ago now, and Donny knew what Maeve was beginning to realise — that the house in Templeogue was only a dream, that the car was falling to pieces with rust, that Liam's money problems were getting worse and that Liam was spending more and more of his time in the pub.

'You'd be better off without him,' Donny said finally. Maeve, holding a cold cloth to her face, said nothing, but when he looked at her, her eyes were brimming with tears. He felt so sad for her then. He sat on the couch beside her and she grabbed him and held him, her tears staining his jeans.

'Oh, Donny!' she sobbed. 'I've really made a mess of things, haven't I?'

Donny was inclined to agree, but he didn't say so. Instead, he searched for something to say that would help, but nothing came. He was remembering his own situation. He had probably just been kicked out of school and he couldn't tell her that. Finally he lied, 'Don't worry, Sis. It'll turn out OK yet. You'll see.' He gave her a friendly nudge. 'C'mon, I'm starving. I'll make you a cup of tea.' Heading for the kitchen, Donny heard the doorbell ring. He looked at the clock. It was five past one. He looked out through the window and saw Bill Moloney's car. He went to the door and stepped outside.

'Hi, Donny,' said Bill.

'Shhh,' whispered Donny, 'she doesn't know anything.' They sat into the car. 'What happened?' Bill asked quietly. Donny told him. Bill listened in silence.

'It's not fair, Sir . . . And it's not right . . . that Sharkey should get away with that!' Bill nodded slowly. His face was grim.

'I know, Donny. It isn't right.' They sat in silence.

'What's the story in school now?' Donny asked finally. Bill looked at him ruefully. 'Well, Sharkey raised the roof when he met the boss. Took him back to the classroom, but of course, you were gone. I haven't had a chance to talk to the boss yet. I know he likes you, but left on his own with Sharkey, the best you can hope for is a transfer down to Shaw Street.'

Donny was shaking his head slowly, fighting back the tears. Much as he complained about it, he liked his school — and it was where all his friends were. The school was run by Christian Brothers though, and even a lay teacher like Bill had little chance of influencing one Brother against another.

'Look, Donny,' Bill went on. 'You know the story. It's very difficult to get a teacher shifted, especially if he's a Brother. You know that.'

Donny nodded. 'It's still unfair!' he blurted out. Bill thought about it for a few minutes.

'OK,' he said at last. 'I'm not going to promise anything, but I'll talk to the boss this evening. I have a few contacts higher up as well. I'll do what I can. At least we've got the holidays coming up, so we'll have time to work something out. Meanwhile, why don't you come over and visit us tonight after you've finished with the papers. Moira's just made that porter cake that you like.'

'OK,' said Donny.

'Have you told Maeve?' Bill asked. Donny shook his head. Bill saw his jaw tighten as he struggled with the anger again.

'He beat her last night,' Donny said tightly. 'I'll kill him if he ever touches her again!'

Bill looked out along the quiet street. A gull swooped low over the terraced houses. The sky was a dull grey. You never know what some of these kids are going through, he thought to himself.

'We'll see you tonight, Donny,' he said. 'Keep your chin up. You're a good lad.'

3

Donny went down to the railway station earlier than usual. He didn't want to meet Flagon and Swamp just yet, not until he had unscrambled the mess in his mind. He walked slowly, wrapped in his own thoughts.

The station was quiet, with few people moving across the wide spaces. Yet Donny had never quite lost the sense of excitement he felt when he first came to work here. This was an enclosed world through which an endless stream of travellers passed. He never tired of looking at them: the dapper businessmen, the hassled mothers, the tired old men, the elegant girls. He wondered where they were going, what their lives were like.

At this time of the evening, however, the station was empty. The tracks stretching away into the grey evening spoke to him of loneliness and something lost. The hollow, metal sounds echoed through the emptiness within him.

Charlie Duggan was sitting at his newsagent's stall, drinking tea from a disposable tea cup. He was surprised to see Donny so early.

'Ah! How'ya, Donny,' he said through a half-masticated cheese sandwich, glancing at the big station clock behind Donny. 'You're early. On the hop from school, eh?'

'Naw,' replied Donny, 'just got fed up and left.'

'Yeh,' said Charlie. 'Pull the other one. It's got bells on it. Here, have a sandwich.' He held out a half-eaten sandwich towards Donny.

'No thanks, Charlie,' he lied, 'never eat cheese.'

Charlie wiped the crumbs from his droopy moustache with his tattooed left arm and dusted his hands on his worn cords. He had long sandy hair, receding at the front, and his freckled face was adorned with a nose that was decidedly flattened. Charlie had once been an all-in wrestler in England and he attributed the shape of his nose to his tactic of trying to beat his opponents by hitting them on the forehead with his face. 'Never failed,' he used to say, a twinkle in his eye.

When Donny finished his paper round, he took another bundle from Charlie and positioned himself on the pavement at the entrance to the station. It was a good position, right next to the traffic lights. Whenever the station was not busy, Donny sold papers to the motorists who stopped at the lights.

The evening rush was just beginning when Flagon and Swamp arrived. Flagon was tall and thin, with a mop of blond hair that looked neat only when it was wet. He was called Flagon because, when he was seven, he marched into the Meteor off-licence with a pound note in his sweaty fist and demanded a 'flagon'. When the assistant didn't give it to him, he kicked up hell, bawling his head off. They only found out later that his old man, whenever he went on one of his alcoholic binges, used to send Flagon out of the house with orders not to return without a flagon of cider, or he'd get the daylights kicked out of him. Flagon did it until one day he was big enough to say no. The old man got such a shock that after that he treated Flagon as an equal, even though he was only fourteen. Apart from his morning milk round, Flagon's main responsibility in life was to collect his dad's wage packet from Conlon's timber yard every Thursday and bring it home to his mother. If they let the old man collect it himself, he'd have it all spent by Friday morning.

Swamp was short and tubby, with a round bespectacled face that belied his razor sharp wit. He didn't talk much, but when he did, you'd have to be sharp to catch the pearls that dropped from his West Dublin accent. His real name was Paul Marsh, but he was affectionately known as 'Swamp', in deference to his surname.

Now he and Flagon stopped beside Donny.

'Hi, Donny,' said Flagon, 'how's it going?' Donny nodded a greeting to them.

'Not the worst,' he replied. Swamp nodded in sympathy. They stood there, awkward, while he sold a paper to a hurrying client.

'Here,' said Flagon, 'give us a few of them.' Donny gave them each a bundle of papers and a fistful of change. Swamp took his to the traffic island and began to sell them to drivers on the opposite carriageway when they stopped at the lights. Flagon canvassed the nearby traffic, while Donny served the station commuters. When Flagon and Swamp were sold out, they came to stand beside Donny again. The ice was broken now. Flagon chuckled quietly to himself. Donny waited.

'I can still see Jaws' face when he came back with the boss,' said Flagon, shaking his head at the good of it. 'Pure livid he was. An' when we told him that you'd done a bunk through the window, he nearly blew a bleedin' fuse altogether!' Swamp smiled in agreement, his eyes sparkling through his thick glasses.

'What did the boss say?' Donny enquired seriously.

Flagon went on. 'Didn't get much chance to say anything. Every time he opened his mouth, Jaws nearly jumped into it! After a while he went on a bit about insolence and insub . . . insub . . . somethin' or other, and lack of respect, and right in the middle of it doesn't Swamp here put up his hand. "Yes Marsh!" roars Jaws. "Excuse me, Brother," says he in this lovely polite voice an' a big innocent face, "Are we getting a half day when we get the Easter holidays tomorrow?"' Flagon doubled over with laughter. 'Jaws nearly had a seizure! Even the boss thought he would, and dragged him out into the corridor.' Donny couldn't contain the smile. He knew they were trying to cheer him up. He stepped over to the kerb to sell a paper to another motorist. When he rejoined the lads, Flagon was kicking at an empty cigarette packet flattened on the pavement.

'I think they sent a letter home to Maeve,' he said, apologetically. Donny received the news in glum silence. Maeve had enough problems, he thought.

'The lads are gettin' up a petition,' Swamp spoke for the first time.

'For me?' Donny asked in disbelief.

'Naw, for Jaws. We want him transferred to Outer Mongolia . . . to teach them Mongonical Drawing.' Donny had to laugh at Swamp's poker face. 'No, seriously,' his friend went on, 'it's for you.'

'Listen Donny,' Flagon broke in, 'we all know he was in the wrong. Even Boloney said it . . . Well, he as much as said it. They *can't* kick you out! Just like that!' Donny didn't believe it, but he nodded anyway. He appreciated the way the lads were standing by him. It made him feel a bit better.

Later, before they left, he agreed to meet them at lunch hour the following day to review the situation.

The rush hour passed. Traffic thinned out. It was nearly dusk. Donny concentrated now on the train passengers. The 7.45 for Galway would leave soon and already he was busy with the first arrivals. After this he could leave.

The evening grew colder. Donny turned up the collar of his jacket and stomped his feet to keep himself warm. He had only three papers left. Then, as he glanced up the street to his right, something caught his eye. Along the pavement on the far side of the street, a man was running towards him. He ran with the waddling gait of a man carrying too much weight, and he looked behind him anxiously as if he were being followed. When he came to the pedestrian lights opposite Donny, they showed red, but the man didn't stop. He scuttled across in front of a blaring truck to the island in the middle. Then Donny recognised him as Liam, his brother-in-law. 'What the hell's he doing here?' he muttered, his blood rising. Liam shouted something, waving his pudgy hand in entreaty, and ran towards him. His face and neck were red and great beads of sweat stood out on his forehead. A wisp of thinning hair was stuck over his right eyebrow.

'Donny! Donny!' he gasped. 'Jaysus, am I glad to see you! Look, you've got to help me!' He looked wildly up the street in the direction from which he had come, fumbling in his pocket at the same time. 'They're after me, Donny. You've got to take this!' He pulled a square, plastic-covered packet from his pocket and held it towards Donny's hand. Donny drew back instinctively.

'Who?' he asked resentfully. 'The cops?'

'No! No!' Liam wheezed. 'Not the cops! It's Magee and the others. They think I'm rattin' on them!' Donny glanced up the street. On the other side, about two hundred yards from them, he saw two dark figures emerge from an alley-way. Liam's eyes darted after his.

'Jaysus! Here they come!' he moaned. The hunted, animal look in his eyes made Donny hesitate, but he had no time to make up his mind. Liam dropped the packet on the path behind him and ran. Donny instinctively looked back towards the two figures. They hadn't spotted Liam yet, because they stood motionless, scanning the far end of the street. Donny stooped carefully, picked up the packet and stuffed it into his pocket. He saw Liam scuttle into a side street and disappear. For a moment it looked as if he had escaped, but when Donny looked again, he saw the two men begin to run along the edge of the street towards him. When they dashed across through a break in the traffic, he recognised the small man in front. It was Slits Magee. A pang of fear suddenly gripped Donny's stomach, but he forced down the panic and steeled himself to hold his ground. He didn't think they had seen Liam talking to him. He turned up his collar of his jacket even more and sank his head down on to his shoulders. A man in a business suit asked him for a *Herald*. Donny took the pound he offered and fumbled in his pocket for change. The two men were closing fast. He turned his back to them, bracing himself for the conflict, but the pounding feet went past him. Over the businessman's shoulder he saw Slits, sprinting now, holding his Crombie hat on his head with one hand, his short, dapper overcoat buttoned tightly round him. The other man, short but with powerful shoulders under a leather jacket, ran jerkily, his thick legs hobbled by his tight jeans. Donny knew him as Dogs. They turned into the side street after Liam.

'C'mon, sonny,' urged the businessman impatiently. 'I've got a train to catch.'

'Sorry,' muttered Donny. 'Here you are.'

Donny was uncertain what to do next. Liam was his brother-in-law, part of the family, and family had to be stuck up for. But, Donny thought, things were different now. Liam had beaten up Maeve, the one person Donny was closest to, and that changed the rules. It would be good enough for Liam if he got a thumping from Slits and Dogs, he thought grimly. And yet . . . maybe the business was more serious than that. Maybe they would hurt Liam . . . badly. And Donny had a suspicion that, bad and all as he was, Liam still meant something to Maeve. Donny didn't want her to be hurt again. He made up his mind quickly.

He dropped the last two papers by the newsagent's stall and headed down the street after the men, his long legs carrying him in an easy lope. When he turned the corner he was in a narrow street, slicing between the high stone wall of the station on one side, and the red-brick warehouses on the other. The pale street light showed it was empty. Then Donny heard a noise to the right in the alley leading to Rumbricks. It was a cul-de-sac. 'The stupid wally!' he said to himself.

In the gloom he saw dark shapes near the high metal doors. Two men standing; a man on the ground. He saw Dogs put the boot into Liam's ribs. Donny sprinted. He leaped, feet forward, kicking hard into the small of Dogs' back. Dogs grunted and staggered forward. The metal door boomed loudly when he struck. Donny landed on all fours but was on his feet in a flash. Something tumbled onto the ground at his feet. It was the packet. Slits, crouching defensively back against the wall, saw it too.

'There it is!' he yelled at Dogs. They both rushed towards him, but Donny was faster still. He grabbed the packet and sprinted for the street. Yells behind him. Before he turned out of the side street, he glanced behind and saw them coming. 'Christ!' he said to himself. But at least it would give Liam a chance to get away. He dashed through the station entrance, almost knocking over an emerging train driver. Under the vaulted roof the sounds of the city faded. But the wide floor was practically empty except for the stragglers filtering through the gate of Platform 7 to catch the Galway train. Donny looked for Charlie. He was busy with four customers. No help there. He made for the platform gate and slid round behind a large man with a yellow suitcase. Over the man's shoulder he saw Slits and Dogs appear at the entrance and slow to a stumbling halt. Donny pushed past a middle-aged woman laden with shopping bags.

'Sorry,' he said to the ticket checker, 'my sister forgot this.' He held up the packet: 'Be back in a sec.' The man opened his mouth to protest but Donny pushed past him, walking fast, resisting the urge to sprint. On his right was the Galway train. Just before he reached the shelter of the goods train to his left, he glanced back. The two men were heading straight for him. A guard was closing the doors of the carriage nearest him. Donny jumped in through the last open door and turned left down the centre passage between the seats, past the few people putting luggage on the racks over their heads, and into the next corridor where the doors

were. Outside, the guard's shrill whistle blew and suddenly
the train was moving ever so slowly. Donny turned right
and grabbed the door handle. He would still have time to
jump down on the tracks and make off into the gathering
night. But he stopped. There was another train stopped
right alongside and he saw immediately that the space
between was too narrow. The train was gathering speed. He
went to the other door, eased down the window and looked
cautiously back along the platform. Slits and Dogs were
running along beside the rear door of the carriage. Dogs had
his hand on the handle and was trying to turn it. But the
train was going faster now. His stocky legs pumped up and
down. Slits, behind him, was yelling something. Then, in
an agony of relief, Donny saw Dogs stumble and let go the
door handle. When he last saw them, the two men were
hurrying back towards the exit.

4

Donny leaned back against the wall beside the door. His heart was thumping and his legs felt shaky. 'Christ' he whispered. Beneath his feet the metal wheels ground on polished rails. He looked out through the window again but the jumble of disused rails and scattered sleepers now speeding past in the dim light from the carriage convinced him that jumping off the train was out of the question. He braced himself against the sway of the carriage and tried to clear his mind. This train, he knew, didn't stop until it reached Athlone, almost eighty miles and an hour and a half away. So he was stuck on it. He had a bad feeling that he had got himself mixed up in something very big and very dangerous. He looked at the packet still in his hand. It was light, weighing no more than a half pound, and whatever was in it yielded to the pressure of his fingers. Two thugs wouldn't go to such lengths to get hold of it unless it contained something of great value. His eyes widened as the realisation came to him. Cocaine or heroin! He stared at it, his feelings in turmoil. How could he have been so stupid! His anger grew. So this was what Liam was into now. Donny had seen the junkies in the park and the pushers in the discos and he knew what the stuff could do to people.

His first impulse was to fling the packet out through the window. Liam could go look for it there. But he didn't do it. He knew that by going to help Liam he had become involved in a dangerous game and he might need this packet as a ticket to get himself out of it. He put it into his jacket pocket.

Now Donny had more immediate problems. He decided that Liam would have had time to get away before the heavies got back to him. Then he found himself wondering what Slits and Dogs would do next. 'Oh shit!' he said aloud. They knew where Liam lived. What if they called on Maeve? Donny shuddered to think what might happen.

He thought then about going to the train guard and telling his story. The more he thought about it, the more far-fetched the story seemed. And even if the guard believed him, you could bet he'd have the police waiting for Donny at the next station. Donny knew enough about the mechanics of police work to realise that if he admitted to receiving a packet of cocaine from his brother-in-law he would almost certainly end up in the nick. And that was one place Donny did not want to be in. No, he would have to wait until the train stopped, get off and phone Bill Moloney. Bill would know what to do. Donny cursed Liam again under his breath. He hadn't paid the phone bills, so the phone company had disconnected the phone at home. That meant he couldn't contact Maeve directly.

Donny now set his mind to the immediate task of getting to Athlone without a railway ticket. Through the wall at his back he heard the rumble of a toilet cistern flushing. He could always lock himself in the jacks when he saw the ticket collector coming. More hassle! Then he remembered a story Swamp had once told about a friend of his who had been in the same fix that Donny was in and how he had procured a ticket for himself. The plan took shape in his mind. He waited.

Soon afterwards, the carriage door slid open and a youth not much older than himself wandered past. Several women came and went before a portly man with an ample midriff trundled out from the carriage. Donny noted the pin-striped suit, the well-fed jowls and the slim briefcase. The door of the toilet closed behind him. Donny gave him a full twenty seconds before he moved. He quickly looked up and down into the two carriages on either side. The coast was clear. Then he knocked sharply on the toilet door and in the deepest voice he could muster said, 'Ticket, please.' He waited a moment, putting his head close to the door. 'Just push it out underneath the door, sir, if you wish.' He primed himself for flight, in case the door opened. There was a muffled response from inside and, a moment later, a ticket slid out under the door. Donny couldn't believe his eyes, but he wasted no time. He picked up the ticket and walked casually into the second carriage, looking straight ahead of him. He went right through and into the narrow roaring corridor. He had put three carriages between himself and the portly gentleman in the toilet when he finally eased himself into a seat in an empty section. Across the aisle a young couple held hands across the table and gazed into each other's eyes. Donny smiled at his reflection in the window and settled down to wait.

At first he didn't feel too good about what he had done, but he consoled himself by reflecting that the ticket collector would be much more inclined to believe an indignant business man than a denim-clad teenager with a Dublin accent and a peculiar story about drugs and street mafia. His guilt soon evaporated.

In the blackness outside the window, a distant light floated away from him. Beyond and behind the train, the glow in the eastern sky spoke of Dublin, now moving away from him at over fifty miles per hour. Donny chuckled quietly to himself. In his mind's eye he could already see Flagon and Swamp gawking at him with open mouths while he recited his story to them. He could see the disbelief on their faces. Cool! he thought.

In the seat behind him a woman was complaining in a hard, low voice about her husband. Snatches of conversation floated through the air. A steward carrying sandwiches and coffee on a tray passed jerkily and Donny realised that he was ravenous. He thought of Moira Moloney's porter cake and his mouth watered. He wouldn't taste any of that tonight, he told himself ruefully. He wished he was already in Athlone so that he could ring Bill. That would ease the anxiety he felt about Maeve. He had told her he would be home before he went up to see Bill and Moira. Now she would be wondering where he was. Once he had rung Bill, he decided, he would head straight out the Dublin road and thumb his way back to the city.

'Ticket, please!'

Donny looked up in surprise to see a small, sharp-nosed man in guard's uniform and peaked cap, staring down at him. He fished in his pocket for the ticket and handed it over, fixing his eyes on the prominent wart under the man's left eye. The other took it and studied it. He turned it over slowly and studied the back of it.

'How far 'you going, sonny?' he asked casually. Donny's eyes dropped to the ticket. With alarm he realised that he hadn't looked closely at it. Was it for Athlone or Galway? He stalled.

'As far as it goes,' he said easily. The guard kept staring at him, but his hand enclosed the ticket so that Donny couldn't see it.

'How far is that?' he asked quietly. Donny took a chance.

'Galway,' he guessed.

'You a student, then?'

At the last second Donny spotted the trick.

'No,' he lied. 'Wish I was. Could get to see me granny on the cheap, then. Couldn't I?'

The other ignored the question. His close-set eyes narrowed even further. 'Where does your granny live, sonny?' he enquired stonily. Donny knew only one place in Galway.

'Salthill,' he said. The guard grunted once and fixed Donny with a thoughtful glare, his head nodding up and down slowly. Donny stared right back, his heart beating a tattoo on his ribcage. But the guard wasn't finished yet.

'How much did the ticket knock you back, sonny?'

Donny knew he had the guard on the run, so he didn't let the last question rattle him.

'It's written on it, isn't it?' he enquired, trying to keep the snottiness out of his voice. It was on the tip of his tongue to ask the unfortunate man could he not read, but he knew that would be stretching the limits of civility to breaking point, so he resisted the urge.

After what seemed like an age, the guard handed the ticket back to him.

'Thanks,' said Donny. He put it in his pocket and looked out the window. But the man didn't move.

'Something wrong?' Donny asked, getting irritated now.

'Oh, no. Nothing wrong,' the other replied with exaggerated politeness, ' — yet.' And he moved away. Donny was relieved. He knew that the guard had him spotted but that he couldn't prove anything. He checked his watch. 8.40. He'd be glad when he reached Athlone.

5

It was nearly forty minutes later when Donny noticed the rhythm of the wheels beginning to slow again and the train began to pass the outlying lights of a town. For some unexplained reason it had stopped for nearly twenty minutes in the isolation of the countryside while Donny had drummed his fingers on the table in annoyance. Now a high embankment carried the tracks around the northern fringe of the town and a jumble of streets and dark-roofed buildings took shape to the south. They passed a high bulk of sheds close at hand and then the regular, well-lit streets of a housing estate. Then the town seemed to end, as massive metal girders loomed outside the window. Donny shaded his eyes from the carriage lights. Far below he saw dim reflections moving and he knew he was crossing the Shannon, Ireland's longest river. Then the hollow sound beneath the wheels became solid, the girders vanished, a stone-flagged platform took shape beneath the window and the train screeched to a stop.

Donny stepped down onto the platform and began to follow the sprinkling of passengers towards the exit. The tension was loosening in him. All he had to do now was to hand over the ticket to the collector and he would be out on the streets of the town. He clutched the packet tightly inside the pocket of his jacket.

He was still about twenty yards from the platform exit when something began to happen there. A woman who was about to go through the doorway suddenly stepped hurriedly to one side, dragging a small child out of the way. Two men rushed past them onto the platform and Donny froze, shock smashing into his stomach. It was Slits and Dogs.

Donny was half turned before they saw him. He heard the shouts but he was already sprinting. His sneakers gripped the flags and he drove for the darkness at the end of the platform. When it abruptly ended he leaped down into the blackness, landing on the ballast beside the tracks. For an instant he heard the sound of hard leather beating on the platform behind and then he had plunged into the night. He stepped into a hollow in the rough stones and went sprawling but he was on his feet in an instant. Glancing behind, he saw Dogs standing on the edge of the platform and he thought he was safe, but something was bobbing in the darkness between, and he knew it was Slits. Fear gave him added strength. He leaped in and ran on the bedded sleepers between the rails where the surface was less bumpy, lifting his feet higher to avoid tripping and falling again. Now he was between the great iron girders and he felt for a moment the emptiness beneath the bridge, where the black river lurked. When the girders stopped he saw below him, to his right, an empty car park and, beyond it, a road running away from the tracks towards the town. The embankment sloped steeply downwards. He searched and found a narrow path through the weeds, slipping and sliding to the wire fence at the bottom. He dipped through the ragged hole in the fence, leaped onto the tarmac of the car park and, in a moment, was on the road and racing for the town. A quick look over his shoulder told him that he wasn't being followed, but he kept running until he came to the shadowy gateway of an old church. There under the overhanging trees he stopped to get his breath. Behind him the street was empty under the lamps.

Donny waited for the tumult inside him to settle. He felt pleased that he had outwitted the two men again, but the satisfaction was tainted by the realisation that they must have driven like madmen down from Dublin in a car, that they wanted the packet very badly, and that Donny was the one who was preventing them from having it. He had seen what happened to someone who displeased the drug barons. Only a month previously, a kid from Donny's neighbourhood had foolishly tried to rip off the local pusher. They found his body in the park, pumped full of heroin. There was only one thing to do, he decided: find a telephone and talk to Bill Moloney.

He buttoned his jacket against the cool night air and set off along the street, hugging the shadows. An old man with a limp pointed him in the direction of a telephone. 'Around the corner to the left,' he said. 'Ye can't miss it.' Donny was wary of cars now. Whenever he heard one coming he stepped into the darkness of a doorway or alleyway until it had passed. He knew Slits and Dogs hadn't finished with him yet.

The telephone kiosk was at the next junction. It was one of those ones with glass on three sides and Donny didn't like it. He would be too exposed in it, like a fish in a bowl. Yet the door faced away from the centre of town and so the wall on which the phone hung would give him some cover if the men were to come from that direction.

He fished five ten-pence pieces from the newspaper money in his pocket, put them in the slot and dialled. His watch read 10.05. Bill would still be up. He heard the ringing tone. A car came slowly from the town centre and he huddled close to the inside of the kiosk. 'Come on!' he urged the telephone. The car passed. A click. Moira's voice. 'Three, seven, oh, five, two, six,' she said. 'Hello.'

'Hello, Mrs Moloney. This is Donny. Is Bill there?'

'Donny!' she said in surprise. 'Where've you been? We've been expecting you since nine thirty.'

Donny was watching the traffic as he spoke. Several cars were coming.

'I got caught in something,' he said. His third ten-pence piece clanked into the box. 'Could I speak with Bill, please?' Moira, sensing the urgency in his voice, called her husband. 'It's Donny,' he heard her say. The cars passed and went on.

'Hello, Donny,' Bill said. 'Where are you?'

'Listen, Mr Moloney. I'm in a bit of trouble. Believe it or not, I'm in Athlone.'

'Athlone!'

'Yeh, Slits Magee and a guy called Dogs are after me.' He told Bill about Liam and the packet and how he had been forced to jump on to the train. 'Listen, I'm worried in case they call on Maeve . . . There may be more of them. Would you mind . . . .' He paused. A car was coming . . . fast. He hugged the corner. Then a silver coloured BMW passed very close to the kiosk, its left indicator flashing. Tyres squealed as it swung round the corner. Donny glimpsed the unmistakable profile of Dogs in the passenger seat. 'Hang on!' he called into the phone. Had they seen him? The car had travelled nearly fifty yards before the brake lights flashed on suddenly. When Donny saw the reversing lights come on, he knew the answer.

'Have to go! They've spotted me!' he shouted. He burst out through the door, leaving the phone dangling. Panic was rising in him. He must get out of sight. Across the street a high wall flanked the footpath, but at the end of the wall he saw the dark opening of an alleyway. He aimed for it. Just before the shadowy entrance swallowed him, he saw the wall beside him light up as the headlight beam swung across it. The alleyway ran between tall buildings and swung to the left after a short distance. Now he could see distant lights. Then suddenly he was out of the narrow passage and his feet sounded on wooden planks. Beneath him was water. He choked down an animal sound that rose in his throat. In horror he realised that he had run into a cul-de-sac. He was on a wooden jetty that ran out across the water for about fifteen yards. Another section joined it there at right angles forming a T-shaped wharf to which three large cruisers were moored. Beyond them was only black, shimmering water. The river! Behind him he heard the screech of brakes.

'Oh God!' he prayed. He would have to act quickly. He turned left at the junction, past the black converted barge and ran towards the sleek, white cruiser at the end. There was no sign of life on board, so he stepped quietly over the chrome rails on to the side deck, and padded round until the cabin shielded him from the alleyway. He knew he was caught. Below him, the water swirled, black and ominous. It flashed across his mind that he should give himself up now, offer the two men the packet in return for his own safety, but just as quickly he knew that it wouldn't work. He had made plenty of trouble for them and he would have to pay.

Donny measured with his eye the fifty yards of black water which lay between him and the bridge, just downstream of him. It was dangerous, but he would have to do it. He looked down along the side of the cruiser. He could make out an object hanging just above the water's edge. Then, somewhere behind him, footsteps came pounding onto the wharf. Donny eased his feet over the side, feeling for the hanging fender. His face was close to the cabin window. And suddenly the light inside came on, the curtain parted, and a young face appeared at the window. In desperation Donny made frantic signs to it. He pressed his fingers to his lips, his eyes wide with a wordless plea. Then he lowered himself over the side. The cold water made him gasp, but he gritted his teeth. The fender, a fat bulbous affair, was tied up at both ends so that it hung horizontally. Donny found that, by holding onto the rings where the ropes were tied to it and lowering himself until he hung beneath it, he was effectively screened from the view of anybody standing on the side-deck above. The water only came up to his neck. He decided against swimming. He would hold on, and take his chances.

He strained his ears to hear above the swirl and gurgle of water around him. A truck powered across the bridge nearby, blasting exhaust into the night air. Then Donny heard the footsteps again. The wooden planks of the wharf creaked under their weight. Somewhere to his left, he heard a hard, metallic clicking and he knew that someone was walking on the iron deck of the barge which was moored nearby.

It seemed an age before Donny felt himself being lifted slightly out of the water as a sudden weight on the other side rocked the cruiser gently. The steps were very near now. He gritted his teeth against the ache in his arms, trying to still his breath and freeze his body so that it would make no sound. The cruiser tilted again and he felt the water creeping up along his neck. The feet were directly above him. He clenched his hands tighter on the ropes, hoping their whiteness wouldn't give him away. He heard a knocking sound, then a movement inside the craft and Slits' voice, unmistakably Dublin.

'We're de p'lice, young f'lla. We're lookin' for a bloke thar excaped from de p'lice car . . . an' he's very dangerous. You didn't happen to norice anyone comin' onto de . . . to de quay here in the last few minutes?' Donny closed his eyes and prayed, steeling himself for the answer. There was a pause. Then a young voice said, 'No. I didn't. Nobody came near this boat anyway.' The voice was strong and clear. There was another pause. Slits was thinking.

'We'll just have a look around anyway . . . Just in case. Dis fella is very dangerous, ya know.'

'OK,' replied the other.

The two men began to search the cruiser. Donny was only dimly aware of the thumping and knocking inside. He was in agony, his mind now focused only on the pain in his arms, forcing his hands to hold on for a few minutes more.

At last the feet stepped again on the deck above him, moved slowly round to the bow and stepped off onto the wharf. When they faded into the distance, Donny knew he must get up now or it would be too late. He had a sudden sensation that the water was pulling him downwards into a black abyss, but he shook it from his mind.

He took a deep breath, dipped his head under water and, as he came up, he hoisted with all his remaining strength. He grabbed for the edge of the deck. His fingers reached it, but they slipped off again and he nearly lost his grip on the rope as he plunged downwards. In desperation he gathered himself for the next effort. This time, he hauled down on the rope until he got his knee on top of the fender. Steadying himself, he became aware of a slight figure kneeling on the deck above him. He felt a hand gripping his collar and lifting. He made a final lunge, and in a moment he was lying face down on the deck, legs dangling, exhaustion giving way to relief.

'Thanks,' he whispered to the figure standing over him. 'Thanks for saving me.' The other didn't speak. Donny pulled himself up to sit on the side deck, resting his back against the cabin wall, and looked up at the slight figure silhouetted against the wharf light. As far as he could tell, the boy was younger than himself, but the woollen cap pulled far down over his ears made it difficult for Donny to see his face clearly.

'Are they gone?' he whispered. The other glanced towards the alleyway. He nodded his head. Donny felt he owed some explanation.

'They're not policemen,' he said quietly. The boy nodded.

'I didn't think they were,' he replied. Donny searched for words to express his gratitude.

'Listen,' he said. 'I think it was great . . . what you did just then. Those guys mean business . . . .' Something near the alleyway caught the boy's eye. He ducked his head suddenly. 'They're there again,' he whispered. 'Quick! Into the boat!' He moved backwards towards the sliding door of the cabin, while Donny crawled on hands and knees after him. He slid, head-first, down the two steps onto the floor of the centre cockpit. To his right, steps led down to another cabin, lit by a weak light. The boy slid the door shut and Donny heard the bolt slide home.

'Don't move!' whispered the boy. They listened. The wharf outside the window creaked again under the heavy weight, but the steps were barely audible. In the darkness of the cabin Donny saw the shadows moving past the curtains towards the end of the wharf. He knew the men were puzzled. They had obviously gone to search for him along the quay near the bridge, thinking that he might have swum away from the wharf. Now they thought he was still on the wharf. They weren't giving up. And that scared him.

After several minutes the shadows passed the window again. The footsteps faded. The boy, watching through a break in the curtains, turned to Donny.

'They've gone,' he whispered. Donny saw the wide frightened eyes in an oval, girlish face. 'What will you do?'

'They won't hang around for long,' he said with a confidence that he didn't feel. 'After they go, I'll just scarper off and get back to town.' The wide eyes devoured him.

'Don't be scared,' Donny said. 'You're OK. I'm on the level. Honest!'

'Why were they chasing you?'

'I've got something they want,' he replied, feeling in his pocket for the packet. He didn't want to have to tell the boy what he thought was in it. He might get the wrong idea. But the eyes were interested now.

'What is it?' he asked, and Donny knew he owed it to the boy to tell him.

'Well,' he said. 'Those men were pushers. And I got . . . was given, a packet. I think there's drugs in it. They want it. That's all.' The other's eyes widened.

'But why don't you go to the police?' he enquired. Donny didn't answer. Instead he stood up. He was beginning to shiver with the cold now and his runners squelched when he moved. The boy sensed his discomfort.

'Oh! But you're soaking,' he said. 'I'll get some dry things. Hang on here a minute!' He indicated the lighted cabin beside Donny and turned towards a door that led forward.

'No. Stall it a minute,' said Donny in alarm. 'Where are you going?'

'There's some old clothes of Dad's in the locker in here. He only uses them when he's working on the engine.'

'Is he in there?' Donny hissed.

The boy smiled and shook his head.

'Of course not. He's at the pub with Veronica. They won't be back until closing time.' Donny let him go and went down into the aft cabin. He was feeling a little warmer now, and when he looked out through a gap in the curtains and saw that the wharf was still deserted, he began to relax a little. The cabin was small but the carpet and wood-panelled walls made it seem very cosy. There were two bunks: one along the back wall and the other under the side window. Donny noted that this second bunk projected into a sort of tunnel which ran through the cabin wall and under the floor of the centre cabin. He was admiring the wardrobe and wash-basin when the boy returned. Donny remembered he hadn't asked him his name.

'I'm Donny O'Sullivan,' he offered, turning towards the other. In the brighter light he could see more clearly. The boy's blue woollen cap concealed all but a few strands of fair hair and the plaid jacket seemed, at first glance, too big for his slim frame. But Donny was startled when he looked into the wide, blue eyes. The boy had a fine, delicate face: he even reminded Donny of a girl he had once seen in the movies.

'I'm Jacky Anderson,' the boy replied. 'Here. Try these on.'

Donny stopped staring and took the bundle of clothes. There were socks, underwear, a shirt, sweater, and pants that smelled mildly of diesel oil.

'OK, thanks,' he said. 'I'll send them on to you, if you give me your address before I go.' Jacky had gone back into the dark centre cockpit again.

Something was bothering Donny about Jacky and he wasn't exactly sure what it was. But he had no time to think about it now, so he put it to the back of his mind as he hurriedly dressed.

The underwear was too big for him, but he didn't mind too much because at least it was clean and dry. When he pulled up the zip of the trousers, however, he found, to his dismay, that the waistband had been designed for a midriff much more ample than his and the legs were too long.

Bleedin' sack! he thought to himself, as he threaded his own belt through the loops and hauled in the folds tight around his waist. He was turning up the leg bottoms when he heard Jacky moving in the other cabin.

'Are you dressed, Donny?' he called quietly. 'They're coming.'

'Who?' he asked, frantically tying up the laces of his wet runners.

'Dad and Veronica!'

'Jeez!' said Donny. 'What'll I do?'

'Nothing,' said Jacky, coming to the cabin door. His eyes sparkled in amusement when he saw Donny's gear. 'I won't say a word. They won't see you.'

'But . . . .'

'Just stay here till things quieten down. They won't come in.' The door closed.

Donny could hear the footsteps on the planked wharf now. They were very close. He padded quickly across the floor and dived for the tunnel at the foot of the side bunk, pulling his legs in after him.

The boat rocked under the new weight and then the steps sounded directly above him on the side deck. Two people walked around to the door. Donny heard it sliding open and then a man's voice. 'Hi, honey. Everything OK?' Donny braced himself for the answer.

'Oh, yes. I've nearly finished that book,' Jacky said in an off-handed way. A woman's voice, more effusive. 'Jacky, darling, why aren't you in bed? You'll catch your death of cold, you know. You're not used to roughing it like this.'

The man interrupted. 'Now, Veronica, Jacky's not as delicate as all that . . . and anyway, it's not a cold night. Come and have a night-cap with us, dear.'

The voices became muffled as they moved into a cabin further forward. Donny relaxed. He crawled out and peered through the curtains. The wharf was deserted. He resisted the impulse to creep away immediately. Instead he lay down on the bunk. He was weary. His mind tried to impose some order on the frantic events of the past few hours. It seemed like ages since he had been talking to Flagon and Swamp outside the station. He remembered how *normal* it had been, in spite of the incident with Jaws earlier in the day. That was Mickey Mouse stuff, compared with the nightmare he was in now. And it had all started with Liam. As soon as that waster came on the scene, Donny thought bitterly, everything began to go haywire. He reached out his hand to touch the smooth plastic of the wall beside him. Outside, the fenders creaked against the wharf. No, it was real all right; he wasn't dreaming. He really was on a strange boat on the Shannon, in the company of a strange boy who had taken a considerable risk for Donny, and of a couple whom he had never even met and who didn't realise that he was a guest aboard their craft. And, as if that wasn't bad enough, he knew that Dogs and Slits weren't far away. They knew he was cornered, or drowned, and he felt an awful certainty that they wouldn't leave until they were sure of him.

Donny felt fairly safe where he was, as long as Jacky didn't spill the beans, so he would stay. He would outwait them. And, in the meantime, Bill Moloney would surely have phoned the police. Even now, the Athlone police were probably looking for him and the two heavies. He comforted himself with the knowledge that it would be only a matter of time before Slits and Dogs would be spotted and picked up, especially if they were hanging around the entrance to the alleyway. So he would wait.

The lights reflecting off the water made faint wavy patterns on the curtains and on the ceiling where it filtered through the gaps. The water underneath the boat rippled and gurgled softly as it caressed the wharf pilings. Donny dozed off.

6

The vibration woke Donny up. He had been aware of it in half sleep for some time. Now the sound of dull throbbing invaded his senses. He woke with a start, staring at the low ceiling and flowered curtains above his head. Reflected sunlight flickered and danced on the ceiling.

Then he remembered. He looked at the other bunk for Jacky but it was empty, the sleeping bag rolled neatly at one end. Donny swung his legs down onto the floor and parted the curtain slightly. The brightness hurt his eyes. With a shock he realised that the boat was moving. All around was a bright expanse of water and far away, over one hundred yards across the glittering water, he saw the wall of reeds that marked the edge of the river.

Donny was suddenly annoyed. Why hadn't Jacky woken him last night, or at least this morning before they left Athlone? Now he couldn't see any sign of a town. He was out in a wilderness of water and he wouldn't be able to get back to Dublin until God-knows-when!

Just then there was a sound at the cabin door behind him. He dived for the tunnel, tucking his legs in. He heard the door open and close and Jacky's voice, calling quietly, 'Donny, Donny.' He crawled out from his hiding place, but when he looked at Jacky, he recoiled.

'Jeez!' he exclaimed. 'Who . . .? What's going on?'

It wasn't Jacky who stood there, but a girl that looked exactly like him. She had shoulder-length, blonde hair, and her eyes held the same excited sparkle that he had seen in Jacky's eyes last night. And suddenly the truth shot home.

'Jeez!' said Donny again. 'You're a girl!'

She nodded, her eyebrows rising in surprise. 'So I am,' she said. 'Is that a sin?' Donny felt that a great con job had been pulled on him. He'd been tricked.

'But, you were a boy last night. I mean, you pretended to be a boy last night,' he accused her, his voice rising. The girl stepped closer to him, glancing quickly at the closed door behind her, her finger to her lips.

'But I didn't, Donny. I didn't pretend to be a boy.' She could read the annoyance in his face. 'I'm a girl. I was a girl last night . . .' A flicker of amusement crossed her face. Donny turned to look out through the rear window of the cabin.

A frothy wake of turbulence stretched back along the water towards a distant spire on the horizon. He was annoyed with himself for not noticing that Jacky was a girl. It made him feel foolish, and that annoyed him even more. But when he turned to her again and saw the hurt in her face, his annoyance vanished and he felt a pig for being so heartless. This girl had taken risks for him last night when he had been alone and in trouble.

'I'm sorry, Jacky,' he blurted out. 'I didn't mean to . . . be like that. It's just a bit of a . . . surprise, that's all . . . .' He hitched up the baggy pants around his waist. When she looked at them, the smile returned to her eyes. Donny surveyed them. They were green and crumpled and oil-stained and his legs were lost in them. To help him over his embarrassment he put his hands in his pockets and spread out the wide legs. 'Charlie Chaplin rides again, huh?' he said, and then she was laughing. Donny felt better then and as he looked at her, he noticed that the white polo-necked sweater didn't disguise the curves of her body. Her slim, jean-clad legs were unmistakably female. He shook his head again in disbelief.

'I just can't believe it,' he said.

'That I'm a girl?' she enquired impishly.

'Well, yeh . . . But more. That I didn't *notice* last night. I mean . . . it's not as if I've never seen a girl before.'

'Well, you must admit I was well camouflaged,' she retorted, laughing.

'Yeh, I suppose so. That old woollen cap covers a multitude . . . No! No! I didn't mean it like that,' he added hastily. 'Your hair is . . .' He wanted to say 'lovely' or 'beautiful' but he couldn't. '. . . OK.'

'Well, thank you,' she said, in mock indignation. 'You do say such nice things to girls sometimes.' He could feel the flush creeping up his face.

'I know!' he exclaimed, remembering. 'When Slits knocked on the door, he called you "young f'la", and, well . . . I just naturally thought . . .' Jacky nodded, her smile showing that she understood. 'It's OK, Donny,' she laughed. 'I forgive you.' He was relieved, but the mention of Slits stirred the anxiety in him again.

'Yeh . . . well . . . anyway,' he continued, 'things have kinda changed now. I mean, what's happenin'? Where are we going? How come you let me sleep all through the morning?'

Jacky went to lock the door. Then she swung her hair back with a practised flick of the head and sat down on the end bunk.

'Don't worry. I've got it all planned. When we get to Aunt Julia and Uncle Dan's place, we'll just wait till the coast is clear and then I'll row you over to the cove and you can thumb back to Dublin from there in safety.' Donny opened his mouth to object but she cut him short. 'Those two men are still waiting at the entrance to the wharf . . .'

'Hold on! Hold on! You're going too fast!' Donny broke in. 'What d'you mean, still waiting?'

'Well, first of all, they came back to the boat looking for you last night.'

Donny started in alarm. 'You mean, a second time?' She nodded.

'Yes. They knocked at the door again and Dad answered it. They told him they were detectives from Dublin and that a dangerous criminal had been seen running onto the wharf and that they were worried in case he might be aboard.' Donny was breathless with suspense. She went on, 'Well, Dad just asked me . . . and I said that I'd seen and heard nothing — except that I was sure I had heard footsteps on the metal barge in front of us just before they'd arrived on the wharf the first time.' She shrugged her shoulders. 'That was it. They swallowed it, and went away.'

Donny rubbed his black hair down over his eyes in a gesture of astonishment, and stared at the blue eyes and lovely face of the girl in front of him.

'Jeez! That's far out!' He didn't try to hide the admiration in his voice. 'But I thought you might have woken me then,' he continued.

'I was going to, but you looked so exhausted I didn't have the heart to. It was just as well anyway.'

'Why?'

'Well, when I went for milk early this morning, they were in the car, sleeping—well, one of them was. And when I got back they were both in the alleyway.'

'Did they say anything?' Donny was concerned now.

'No. They just glared at me suspiciously and I walked past them.' Her eyes were bright with enthusiasm and she drew her knees up in front of her face and hugged them to her. 'It's so exciting, Donny, isn't it?'

Donny could have found more suitable words to describe the scene, but he was too full of wonder and admiration to say anything. He was rapidly revising all his views on girls.

'Anyway,' she continued, starting up from the bunk, 'you must be famished.'

He nodded vigorously. 'Yeh, I could do with a sambo or something.'

'I'll smuggle something in for you,' she said excitedly.

Donny nodded significantly towards the front of the boat. 'Where are the others?'

'Well, Dad's driving, and Veronica . . . I think she's doing the dishes.' Jacky moved closer to Donny, 'She doesn't like getting her poor hands wet, but I wouldn't do them, so she's got to. She wouldn't want Dad to think that she's no good at housework, you see.' Jacky seemed to enjoy the idea of Veronica's doing the dishes. 'Serves her right,' she said as she unlocked the door. 'See you in a sec.'

When she had gone, Donny sat down on the side bunk out of sight of the door and let things settle in his mind. Flagon and Swamp will never believe *this*, he thought. Then, just to prove to himself again that he wasn't dreaming, he jumped up and looked out through the curtains, drawing them wide open. The river had become very wide now, the shores receding on both sides until he could make out the trees along the shoreline only with difficulty. In the hazy distance beyond the lakeside reeds, he saw low, blue hills. A small, tree-covered island slid into view on his right and, almost immediately, to his left, a large white cruiser with green and orange trim went ploughing past, heading for Athlone. A German flag fluttered from the short flagstaff at the stern. Donny watched fascinated as the big bow wave from the other cruiser glided closer and closer. He felt the floor underfoot lift and fall as the wave slid beneath it. This is something else, Donny thought. A wave of exultation swept over him, but he resisted the urge to let go a great whoop of delight. He knew that he wasn't out of the woods yet, but he felt secure in the knowledge that Slits and Dogs were far away.

Donny was brought back to reality when he looked at the door and noticed that he had forgotten to put the bolt on, after Jacky had left. He didn't particularly want to be discovered lurking in Jacky's room. He would have a lot of explaining to do, especially now that he knew that Jacky was a girl. In his mind's eye he could see her dad bearing down on him. 'Would you kindly explain to me why you're wearing my clothes after spending the night in my daughter's bedroom?' Donny shuddered at the thought. It was a long swim to shore and he didn't fancy walking the plank. He crept to the door and fastened the bolt. There was a sliding metal grille set into the door at eye level. He slid it open carefully and peered through. Above and in front of him he saw a wide expanse of Aran sweater stretching between two burly male shoulders. Above that, a dishevelled thatch of greying hair thrust out from under a sailor's cap. Although he couldn't see, Donny knew that the man was holding the wheel, turning it this way and that.

'Shit!' said Donny to himself. He decided that it would be very much in his interest not to be discovered.

Just then, a laden tray appeared suddenly level with his eyes. He eased back the bolt and leapt back into the cabin. Jacky stepped down and closed the door.

'Here,' she whispered, her eyes bright. 'Here's some food.'

'Great!' exclaimed Donny. He wolfed the brown bread and jam hungrily and washed them down with hot tea. Jacky sat watching him, looking as if she couldn't wait for the next episode in the adventure to happen.

'That was great!' said Donny, wiping his mouth with his sleeve. 'Do it all yourself?'

'Oh, no,' she retorted. 'I just gave Veronica your order and told her that Mr O'Sullivan in the first class cabin wanted his breakfast, and hurry up about it.' He smiled ruefully. Even Swamp would have his hands full with this sharp kid, he thought.

'Anyway, what about you?' he asked.

'I've had mine, hours ago,' she replied.

'No. Not that. I mean, what's your story?'

'Not very exciting, I'm afraid,' she said glumly. 'In fact, it's pretty boring.'

Donny looked around the cabin. 'Nice way to be bored, huh?' he remarked. She shrugged her shoulders. 'This? This is all right, I suppose, for a few days. But it's boring when you have no friends along.' She drew her knees up and clasped them to her. 'Dad and Veronica — well they're older, you know. And Veronica gives me a pain. She's so full of airs and graces!'

'She's not your mum, then?' Donny queried.

'Humph! She'd like to be my *new* mum. But over my dead body!' Donny liked her flash of spirit. He wanted to ask her about her own mother but he knew it might touch against the pain in both their lives, so he decided against it.

'Most of my friends are in Dublin,' she continued, 'except a few that I have in school.' Donny's eyebrows shot up at this. 'Boarding school,' she added glumly. 'They send me to boarding school down the country. It's a dreadful dump! Lots of fuddyduddy old teachers. And even the girls are . . . well, soppy . . . except one or two. I hate the place!' Donny believed her. Everyone seemed to be having trouble with school these days. 'I'm going to run away if they send me back after Easter. I am, you know. I told them I would.' She looked at him seriously and Donny reckoned that running away from school would be no big deal for Jacky. 'They're trying to butter me up . . . taking me on a cruise like this, but it won't work. I told them so, but they won't believe me.'

The set of her chin and the flash of fire in her eyes convinced Donny that she meant it. He nodded in sympathy, remembering his own problems. The difference between them was that Jacky was having trouble in getting to go to the school near her home where her friends were, while Donny was going to have trouble in getting to *stay* in the school where *his* friends were. Jacky noticed his frown.

'What is it?' she asked.

'Oh, nothing much,' he said. It occurred to him that it wouldn't do his image with Jacky any good if he told her about the incident with Jaws and about the trouble at home.

'Tell me!' she insisted. 'You've told me almost nothing about yourself. I'd really like to know.' Donny took a deep breath.

'I don't think you'll be very impressed,' he said.

'I will,' she said eagerly. 'I know I will.'

So Donny told her about the previous day, about Maeve and Liam and Jaws and Slits and Dogs and Bill Moloney, and his two mates, Flagon and Swamp. Jacky listened with intense interest, and he knew by her gasps of astonishment that she was indeed impressed.

Donny had just reached the part of the story where he had jumped down onto the tracks at the station in Athlone when there was a delicate knock on the cabin door. The rumble of the engine below drowned the sound of the scuffle Donny made as he dived for the tunnel. He hauled up the mattress after him until it formed a wall across the mouth of the tunnel, and there he waited, holding his breath. He heard Jacky opening the door, and then Veronica's voice, dripping with honey.

'Jacky, darling, you must be quite lonely in here all on your own.'

'Oh, no, Veronica. I've been reading.'

'So I decided I simply must come in and talk to you.' Veronica came down the steps into the cabin. 'You and I have so much to talk about, haven't we?'

'Have we?'

'But of course we have . . .'

Jacky cut her short. 'No, no, Veronica, you sit over here. It's much more comfortable!' Donny felt the bunk move slightly under him as a weight came on the other end. He peered through a crack between the mattress and the roof. Veronica was sitting within three feet of him! He froze.

'Oh, but I don't mind, dear. In fact I like the hard seat,' said Veronica, and Donny caught the scent of perfume. He could see her face clearly now. A long aquiline nose overhung a thin mouth laden with lipstick. Above it all he could see the dark stems at the roots of her rinsed blond hair. Donny gritted his teeth. His nose began to itch unbearably from the perfume on the air.

'All right,' said Jacky with alarming calmness, 'but don't sit where the woodworms are.'

'Oh! Worms! Where?' Veronica leaped up suddenly and began to inspect the bunk and the back of her dress. 'I hate worms. They're nasty little things.' She moved out of Donny's view.

'Oh no, Veronica,' said Jacky firmly. 'They're very useful when you're fishing.'

'Well, I suppose . . .'

'Y'see, you take the fishing hook and you stick it into the worm. You know? Into its guts.' Jacky said the last word with particular relish. Veronica gave a little gasp. 'Oh, please, Jacky. Could we not talk about something a little more . . . well, pleasant?'

'Oh, I'm sorry, Veronica. Am I upsetting you?' asked Jacky ever so sweetly. 'Shall I tell you about the book I'm reading then?' Veronica seemed pleased. Donny was in the early stages of acute claustrophobia.

'Oh, please do,' Veronica said.

'Well, it's about this hunchback, who finds this tomb deep in the swampy jungle. And the tomb goes down deep into the bowels of the earth. And . . . and . . .' Jacky took a long deep breath, 'and it's inhabited by this tribe of creatures from the Beyond. They're all slimy and evil smelling, and they're made out of this horrible stuff called flasma, and they have a horrible smell, like . . . like dead fish, and . . . and in the middle of the night they slither and slide up along . . .' Veronica let out a horrified gasp. 'Yes, well, Jacky. That sounds really interesting. But you must excuse me now. I've got some housework to do, you know?' Veronica gave a shrill little laugh and fled from the room.

When Jacky turned back from locking the door, she found Donny falling around the bunk, in stitches. Then she, too, collapsed with laughter. It took them nearly five minutes to recover. Each time when Donny thought that he was back to normal, Jacky would go through the ghoulish routine again. '. . . an' they'd slither in under the door and slobber their way up the leg of the bed — and on to Veronica's big toe.'

'Listen,' said Donny after a while. 'What's the plan again? How long will it be before we get to where we're going?' He looked out across the lake, duller now that a cloud had hidden the sun.

'They've decided to stop at the hotel for lunch,' Jacky said seriously, 'but that won't be much good to us, because it's on the wrong side of the lake. They won't take very long, though, and then it's only a short journey across the lake to Rabbit Island. Then I'll row you over to the cove.'

Donny's face showed his impatience.

'Well, don't blame me,' she retorted. 'I did the best thing for you. If I'd woken you up, you'd have gone out and those two men would have got you!' The fire was in her eyes again.

'Yeh, I suppose you're right,' he admitted. 'It's just that I'm a bit worried about Maeve. I hope Bill Moloney got the message to her.'

'I'm sure he did,' she said, reassuringly. 'Anyway, things nearly always turn out better than we think they will.'

Before yesterday, Donny might have agreed with that sentiment, but he wasn't so sure now, because his life had taken a drastic turn for the worse, in his opinion. Still, he had to admit that he'd never met anyone in the female line quite like Jacky. She was so *alive* — you couldn't stay down in the dumps for long while she was around. Even now, he was beginning to feel more confident about what lay ahead.

'This island? What's the story about it?' he enquired.

'That's where Uncle Dan — Dad's brother — and Aunt Julia live — and Geoffrey.' A slight frown flickered across her brow at the last name.

'On an island?' Donny was surprised.

'Yes,' she went on, 'they've got a farm there. It's quite large, you know, and they're the only ones who live there. But it's only a short row over to the cove — that's the mainland — and they've got lots of boats. It'll be pimps.' She sparkled again.

'Who's Geoffrey?' Donny had noticed the frown.

'Geoffrey's my cousin,' she said, as if resigned to a very unpleasant fact. 'He's a wally! I'm not sure if he's home from school yet. If he is, we'll have to give him the slip. He's always annoying me — pulling my hair and pinching me. You know the sort?' Donny nodded, smiling.

'Yeh, I think I do.'

'He's a bully, but he's a bit thick really, so we'll have no problem getting rid of him. You'll see.' She brightened again.

Donny didn't really doubt what she said, but he didn't want any hassle either, because he wanted to be back on the road. Now his thoughts turned to his wet gear. He fumbled under the bunk where he had stowed them and hauled them out.

'Any chance of drying this stuff?' he asked. Jacky looked at the hand rails running across the stern of the boat.

'You slip them out through the window and I'll go out and peg them to that.'

'What about them?' he asked, jerking his thumb towards the forward cabins.

'They won't notice,' she scoffed. 'Dad hasn't a clue what sort of clothes I've got, and neither has Veronica. They'll just think they're mine, if they notice them at all.'

Moments later, Donny's jeans, shirt and jacket were flapping in the southerly breeze at the back of the cruiser.

He'd held on to his underwear. He told himself he didn't want to embarrass the girl by asking her to hang them out. He put the change from Charlie's papers and the offending packet — the cause of all his trouble — on the shelf to dry.

7

Not long afterwards, Donny heard the engine sound change and the craft began to slow down. He got up from the bunk, where he had been lying after Jacky had left, and looked out. On the left, the shore was very close now. He saw black and white cows in a field just beyond the fringing reeds. Beyond, the fields sloped gradually upwards to where a cluster of beech trees stood sentinel on top of a low hill. Looking back, in the bright water to the south, he saw another, smaller cruiser ploughing purposefully in his direction. Apart from it, the lake was empty.

The engine slowed further. Then there was a gentle thump somewhere near the front and a timber wharf slowed to a stop beside him. Donny drew the curtains quickly and stepped back into the gloom of the cabin. Footsteps sounded on the side-deck and then a man's feet stomped on the wharf.

Jacky tapped softly on the door. 'I'll be back as soon as I can — I can't get out of it. Don't go out or you'll be seen. 'Bye.' And she was gone.

When the footsteps had faded into the distance, Donny relaxed for the first time since he had woken up. The wharf had been built at right angles to the shore and now, because the bow of the cruiser pointed directly landwards, he couldn't see the hotel from the cabin windows. He opened the cabin door cautiously and stepped up into the centre cockpit where the wheel and controls were. He looked gingerly through the high windscreen. Several large cruisers were moored on either side of the long wharf in front of him. Beyond them he saw four towering fir trees hedged round by smaller bushes and shrubs and, through the foliage, the warm red-brick gable-end of a large building — the hotel. The wharf was deserted.

On the shelf below the windscreen he found a map. He had been considering trying to get to a road, but the map told him that he was several miles from a main road, and it seemed to wander all over the place before finally arriving back at Athlone. He decided to take Jacky's advice and wait until he reached the eastern shore.

He was hungry again. He pushed open another door and looked down into the galley. His eyes lit on a large bowl of fruit resting on a small table. He stepped down and took an apple and an orange, stuffing them into the cavernous pockets of his pants. Then he went back to the centre cockpit to study the controls.

Donny was interested in things mechanical. He had once taken the engine of Liam's old Honda 50 to pieces and reassembled it so that it actually started and kept going. He turned the ship's wheel this way and that now, marvelling at the ease of movement. There was only one control lever, he noted, and he had just concluded that this must control both the gears and throttle when he heard the sound of a craft pulling in behind him. It was a smaller cruiser and the cockpit was at the very rear, covered only by a canvas canopy. Donny watched as it approached the wharf. Too fast! he thought. Too late the helmsman realised it. The engine gave a sudden roar and the bow of the cruiser smacked into the wharf. Donny felt the vibrations run through the floor underneath. He was about to duck down into the aft cabin again when a figure stepped out from under the canopy and vaulted lightly onto the wharf. It was Slits. Donny froze, an iron hand gripping his stomach. When he thought about it later, he knew that he should have opened the sliding outside door and run for it along the wharf towards the hotel grounds. But he didn't. Instead he stepped lightly down into the aft cabin and dived for the bunk. He pulled the light mattress up as he had done before and waited, trying to still his pounding heart.

Footsteps. Hurrying. Someone stepped on to the side deck. Donny held his breath. Was the outside door locked? No sooner had the question formed in his mind than he heard it slide open. Oh Jesus! he whispered. He tensed, ready for action. Slits he could handle, but not both of them. He listened. There was only one set of footsteps. They went forward into the galley. Doors opened and slammed shut. Donny decided to make a run for it. He threw down the mattress and stepped down. The floorboards creaked horribly. He grabbed the door and leaped into the empty centre cockpit. Too late he saw that Dogs was standing on the wharf outside the sliding door. He heard hurried footsteps in the galley and then Slits came rushing up the steps. He was caught. He thought of putting up a fight but then he saw the gun in Slits' hand.

'Yeh, you little shit!' Slits snarled. 'We got you!' Donny saw the gun swing in an arc. He ducked and stepped back all in one movement, but something hard glanced off the top of his skull. A piercing pain.

'Aagh!' Donny yelled. 'Watch it, you scab!' He put his hand to his head. It was sticky and warm.

'Dogs!' Slits called. 'C'mere!' Dogs' head appeared through the doorway and the muscles bunched on his thick shoulders. His fat cheeks almost enveloped his little eyes and he looked expectantly at Slits, flexing his pudgy fingers slowly.

'Get him into the boat!' Slits told him. Dogs turned his red eyes on Donny, looking at him in the way a schoolboy would look at a cream doughnut, with delicious anticipation.

'OK, OK!' said Donny. 'You can have the packet — whatever it is. I don't want it.' Slits looked at Dogs in mock surprise.

'Oh! The little shit-head doesn't want it,' he mimicked. Dogs moved closer to Donny but Slits held out a restraining hand. 'Where is it?' he said quietly.

'It's there, in the cabin,' Donny said, taking a step towards the door.

'Hold it!' yelled Slits. He motioned to Dogs who moved to the steps, all the while watching Donny as a cat watches a mouse. In a moment he was back, handing the packet to Slits. Slits nodded, his little weasel eyes cold and hard.

'Take him!' he said. Donny opened his mouth to protest, but the words never came. Dogs hit him in the ribs just behind his left arm. His innards seized up. The pain was awful and he couldn't breathe. He hit the floor, gagging, wanting to get sick. He felt himself being lifted, pushed through the door onto the wharf. Dogs half-dragged, half-carried him to the other boat and in a moment he was lying on the floor of the main cabin. Slits stepped down after them and Donny saw the pointed shoe coming for his face. He twisted away, bringing his hands up to ward off the blow, but the shoe caught him under the chin and wrenched his head back.

'There's a man in town wants to see you,' growled Slits, 'but one word outta you and you'll never see him.' Donny squirmed away, bracing himself for the next blow, but it didn't come. Through his hands he saw the two men go out to the cockpit and, in a moment, the engine started somewhere at the back. Dogs sat on the side bench just outside the door while Slits cast off, and then the engine increased its revs and Donny knew they were moving away from the wharf. He felt his jaw tenderly. He was furious with himself for letting them creep up on him unawares. He had underestimated them and now he was in the worst trouble of his life.

When Donny had recovered a little, he stood up slowly while Dogs watched him greedily all the while. He knew Dogs was itching to let him have another crack in the ribs and he didn't want to give him an excuse, so he eased himself in on the bench that ran beside the table, facing Dogs. He pretended, however, that he was still hurt, keeping his arms across his stomach and his head down. He had to have time to think.

He knew they were taking him back to Dublin to meet some man, and he had a good idea who that might be: the Boss, the Godfather, a sinister figure in the Dublin underworld whom Donny had grievously displeased. He shuddered at the thought of what might be in store for him there. He would have to escape, and soon.

Dogs' solid frame still filled the opening of the cabin door. He sat sideways now, talking quietly at times to Slits, who was out of sight at the wheel. Donny couldn't hear what they were saying, above the throb of the engine. He looked out past Dogs. Far away across the lake, the cruiser, still clear and white in the sunlight, sat where he had left it, but with each passing second it became smaller and smaller.

Donny glanced around the cabin. There were sliding windows on either side of the cabin, each one probably big enough for him to slide through. But it was useless to think about it while Dogs sat at the door. And even if he did get time enough to squeeze through and dive overboard, he knew that he wouldn't have swum far before they would catch him. And what they might do then didn't bear thinking about. Slits would be just as likely to drive right over him and let the propeller mangle him as to haul him out of the water. He was that kind of man.

Donny had a momentary feeling of panic. 'Oh God,' he prayed, 'get me out of this.' When the cruiser back at the hotel had begun to merge with the shimmering tops of the waves, Donny knew it was useless to hope for any help there. The reality, he had to accept, was that Jacky would find him gone and conclude that he had left the boat to thumb back to Dublin. For her, the great adventure would be over. And for himself, too, he concluded grimly, unless he did something.

Suddenly Dogs stood up from the seat. He turned so that his back was towards Donny, but although Donny held his breath, he didn't move from the doorway. Now the opening was completely blocked. With rising anxiety, Donny saw that the lake was narrowing. They were coming down to the river. Through the window behind him, he saw the spires of Athlone rising above the riverside woods. The boat wound through black and red markers past several wooded islands. Time was running out for him.

Donny knew that he would have to get Dogs away from the doorway. All he needed was enough time to spring to the steps, take two paces across the aft cabin, get one foot up on the bench seat and then he would be down and under the water behind the boat. He measured the distance to the nearest reedbed. Too far, if he wanted to swim underwater. They'd have to be nearer. In the pool back home, he had often swum over thirty metres underwater. But now he had these great baggy pants on. They would slow him down.

The river's edge to his right was getting nearer and nearer now. Donny watched it out of the corner of his eye, the tension gripping him in the gut. Slits was cutting a corner. The reeds were only twenty metres away now. Donny reached over carefully and began to undo the window catch. He had the window half open when Dogs moved again. He whipped back his hand, dipping his head to look at the table. He saw Dogs' feet turn round on the step and he knew that he was looking at him. Then Donny's stomach did a great somersault. Dogs stepped up into the aft cabin. The feet moved back and stopped before the long bench seat. When Donny looked up he saw that there was a narrow, three-foot gap to the left of Dogs, who was staring down at the water behind the boat. Not yet, he told himself.

Dogs turned to the right; the gap widened. Donny took a deep breath and got out from the seat behind the table. He measured the steps with his eye, his heart pounding. Then like a spring being released, he bounded forward. His right foot landed on the top step. He pushed forward, sprang off the left, up onto the cushion on the bench, kicked hard against the gunwale, straightened his body out over the churning water and plunged. In mid-air, he saw the dinghy below and a little to the right. He missed it by inches. Just before the splash he heard a sudden shout behind, and then his ears were bubbling and the cold shock hit his body. He aimed for the bottom, turning right for the reeds at the same time. The water swirled and bubbled in his eyes. Below him was only murky greyness.

He stroked powerfully with his arms, conscious of the pants that wrapped themselves around his threshing legs. He still couldn't see the reeds. 'Oh, Christ!' he thought. 'Where are they?' His air was running out. Gritting his teeth, he forced down the panic and stroked three more times. Then he knew that he would have to surface. As he came up, he saw the stripes in the water ahead. The reeds! He made one last, desperate plunge and then the reeds swam into his face. He parted them, hauled himself into them, and then his head broke the surface. He sucked in air and stroked again, feeling the reeds tugging at his arms and legs. Then he felt the rocks underfoot and plunged through the remaining reeds to the grassy bank inside. He glanced behind. Through the swaying reeds he saw the boat. It was only twenty metres away, steaming directly towards him. Dogs' thick frame stood at the prow, his hand over his eyes, scanning the shore.

Donny ducked his head and plunged into the hazel thicket that grew at the water's edge, arms up to protect his face. Behind him a shout and then a loud report.

'Oh, God!' he thought. 'They're shooting at me!' He burst through the thicket into the open space beyond and sprinted for the bushes on the other side. His foot caught a tuft of matted grass and he fell headlong but sprang up just as quickly and tore through a narrow opening in the thicket. Once through here he would be out of sight and safe for the moment. A glittering through the leaves caught his eye. When he burst out through the last bushes, he stopped in his tracks. A wall of reeds blocked his path, and, beyond them, open water stretching over fifty metres away from him to another shore. Desperately he looked up and down the shoreline where he stood. Then the awful truth dawned on him. He was on an island!

'Oh, Jesus!' he prayed. 'Help me!'

His first impulse was to wade directly in through the reeds and swim for the far shore, but he resisted it. He would be too exposed for too long. Looking left, he saw that the northern point of the island seemed to be closer to the mainland. He ran along the rocky shore towards it, keeping outside the thicket, plunging into the reeds whenever an overhanging branch blocked his way. There was another shout some distance behind and he ran faster. He decided against swimming for it. He didn't want to end up at the bottom of the river with a bullet in his back.

At the north point of the island the thick bed of reeds grew outwards from the shore in a wide arc. They were so thick that Donny couldn't see through them. It flashed into his mind that he could lose himself in them for as long as he wished, once as he didn't leave a tell-tale trail behind him. He glanced behind. Something moved behind an overhanging branch far back along the shore. He ducked his head, watching as Slits pushed through the foliage, coming towards Donny. He heard him shouting and then an answering shout from Dogs, still screened by the trees. Donny crouched and moved around the point of the island to his left before wading carefully into the reeds, straightening the long stalks behind him as he went. The water became deeper. When he reached the outer edge, he found that he could just touch bottom while keeping his head above water. He searched with his foot and found a submerged rock on which to stand, grabbed a bunch of reeds in both hands and waited. The westering sun beat down on the water and, screwing up his eyes to keep the light from hurting them, he scanned the river up and down hopefully for any sign of help. But there were no boats to be seen. His only hope now, he knew, was that if they didn't find him during their first search, they would conclude that he had either swum to the mainland or drowned in the attempt.

It was only when Donny moved a little farther to the left around the point to where the cover was denser, that he realised how narrow the island was. There, only fifty yards away, the stern of Slits and Dogs' cruiser protruded from the reeds. He stared at it for a moment, his mind a ferment of possibilities. Then a crazy thought surfaced. What if they, in their haste to get him, had left the keys on board and the craft unguarded? No, he told himself. That only happens on TV. Far too dangerous anyway. He pushed it out of his mind and concentrated on the cold of his body. He knew he couldn't stay immersed in the icy water for much longer. The freshening wind roughened the surface and little waves began to lap against his shoulders. He wished to God he knew where Slits and Dogs were.

When he glanced in the direction of the cruiser again, what he saw made him plunge suddenly into the reeds. The craft was moving. Relief surged through him as he lowered himself behind a wall of reeds. They were leaving. They had given up. But, as he waited tensely, another, more terrible thought struck him. They were going to search for him from the deck of the cruiser. Caught where he was, he would have no chance. Panic seized him. He scanned the dense hazel thicket ashore for a gap through which he might plunge. He was on the point of making a desperate burst, when he heard the voices again. Incredibly they seemed to come from a point behind the hazels. He listened again. Yes, he was positive. Perplexed, he peered out at the cruiser again. It was now fifteen metres out from the island, drifting slowly towards a point opposite where he stood. A rope trailed down into the water from the prow, where the name 'Firefly' was clearly written in red letters. He saw no sign of life on board. And then the stunning truth struck him. The cruiser had broken free. The men hadn't tied it properly and the wind and waves had sucked it out of the reeds and were pushing it slowly towards him. A desperate plan formed in his mind. Keys or no keys, he knew that he would have a better chance on board the drifting cruiser than he would if he remained where he was, trapped on an island, waiting for the men to come. But he would have to act immediately.

The craft was drifting faster now and he knew that if he waited for it to reach a point opposite where he now was, he might not be able to swim fast enough to catch it. He made a sudden decision. Listening first for any sound along the shore, he stood on tip-toe, parted the long reeds and scanned the thicket. It was a dense wall. Then he struck out for a point about fifteen metres north of the drifting craft, swimming powerfully in his favourite overarm stroke. His heart pounded with fear. At any moment the men might emerge from cover and shoot him while he swam. The boat was moving faster now and he had to adjust his aim. The wind blew stronger on the open water. In desperation he realised that he mightn't make it, that the boat might drift past him and he would be unable to catch it. He redoubled his efforts, but the flappy pants slowed him. The white hull floated closer. Now it was passing. Desperation spurred him on. He saw the rope hanging from the bow, trailing in the water. He closed his eyes and lunged for it. His hand touched something pliable and then it closed on the rope. He hauled himself along it until he was directly under the bow. Nearly exhausted, he wrapped the rope around him and held on. He had made it!

Suddenly there was a shout from directly behind him on shore. He twisted just in time to see Slits bursting out from the hazels on the point, closely followed by Dogs. They stopped short, hands shading their eyes, staring at the boat, now forty metres from them. Slits turned abruptly to Dogs and began taking off his coat. When he bent down out of sight, Donny knew that he was taking off his shoes. He didn't see Slits clearly again until he came surging through the last line of reeds and began swimming towards him, his arms rising and falling in a short stabbing action that seemed to haul him through the water at a terrific speed. Donny tried to pull himself up along the rope to the prow, but the strength hadn't returned to his arms yet. He let go the rope and swam round to the starboard side. A blue fender hung down almost to the water's edge. He grabbed it and, using his knees, he hauled himself up onto the side deck. He had a sensation that he was reliving something that had happened to him before. When he stood up on the side deck, Slits was only twenty metres from the boat, his black hair clinging to his skull, arms flailing as strongly as before.

Donny looked down into the cockpit. His heart leaped when he saw the keys still in the ignition. He jumped down and grabbed the red gear lever, pushing it forward. In an agony of suspense he turned the key clockwise. Somewhere underneath the floor the engine began to turn over sluggishly. Donny felt the craft move slightly forward. It's in gear, he thought. He pulled back on the red lever and tried the ignition again. This time the engine surged into life. Through the windscreen Donny saw Slits' twisted face only five metres from the starboard side. He rammed the red lever forward. There was an answering surge of sound and power and the boat lurched forward. Donny spun the wheel frantically towards open water, pushing harder on the lever. Slits grimaced with effort, clawing at the fender as it swept past him, but he missed it. Elated, Donny turned to look back at him. But his joy was short-lived. The dinghy tied behind the boat swung across, Slits made a final plunge and grabbed the side of it, and, in a moment, its nose shot upwards as Slits hauled himself in over the stern. His black hair was plastered down over one eye and he mouthed horrible obscenities as he struggled to gain his balance in the swaying dinghy. Donny let go the wheel and rushed for the stern cleat to which the dinghy rope was tied. Slits, reading his mind, jumped over the dinghy seat, tripping in his anxiety to get to the other end of the rope. He recovered, grabbed the rope and began to haul the dinghy furiously towards Donny. Frantically, Donny tore at the knot, but he couldn't get it to open.

'You bloody little shit!' yelled Slits. 'Get away from there! You're dead! You hear! Get away!' Realising that he wasn't going to succeed, Donny let go and glanced around the cockpit. A pair of oars lay on the floor. He grabbed one and straightened up just as Slits' hands reached the back of the cruiser. He aimed the heavy oar handle at Slits' right hand. It landed with a solid 'thunk', but Slits was too fast. Donny jumped up onto the rear seat, desperation giving him a savage strength. He swung the oar in a wide arc. It came all the way from behind his shoulder. Too late, Slits saw it coming. With a curse, he released his grip on the transom and raised his left arm to ward off the blow. The oar caught him across the ribs just below the arm. Donny felt the solid shock through his hands and heard the sharp grunt from Slits. Slits fell sideways across the dinghy, but his right arm saved him from pitching overboard. He scrambled to his feet, poising himself to grab the rope again, but the dinghy, now no longer held close to the cruiser by Slits, drifted back. Then, suddenly, the rope tautened. Slits, caught by surprise, pitched backwards into the dinghy. He landed on his butt, feet in the air and Donny heard a solid thud as his head whacked off the rear seat. Dropping the oar, Donny dived for the knotted rope again. This time his hands were less frantic and in a moment the rope came free. He didn't let go immediately, however, because a sudden surge of fury welled up in him against two men who were trying so single-mindedly to destroy him.

'You stupid little runt!' he yelled at Slits, still sitting dazed on the floor of the dinghy, holding the back of his head painfully. 'You an' that great fat bulldog of yours! You can wait for Sealink now . . . !' He stopped short because he suddenly realised that the cruiser had swung almost full circle and was bearing down at full speed on the shore of the island, near where Dogs stood transfixed. Donny dropped the rope and leaped over to the controls. He swung hard on the wheel and the bow swung to the right, away from the island. Behind him, Slits was shouting. Donny heard only three words, but they chilled him to the bone.

'. . . sister is dead . . . !' He looked back at Slits, who mouthed the words again. 'Your sister is dead, O'Sullivan!' Then he turned and shouted something at Dogs. When Donny saw Dogs' stance, he knew that he was aiming a gun in his direction. He ducked into the cabin, still holding the wheel in his left hand. There was a sudden sharp explosion behind him and a shower of window glass sprayed over the table and floor. Donny crouched tensely by the door, only pushing the wheel over a little to take him farther from the island, not daring to look back until he was sure that he was out of range.

When, a few minutes later, he did peer around the bulwark, he saw that Dogs was no longer interested in him. Instead, he was moving along the shore towards a point opposite where Slits and the dinghy still floated. Slits was lying across the prow of the craft, paddling awkwardly with his hands, trying to keep a straight course for the island.

8

It was several minutes before the tightness in Donny's stomach began to relax. During this time he kept the cruiser, Firefly, at full throttle, its prow pointing northwards straight up the lake. His anxious glances behind showed that Slits was now safely back on the island, but Donny could see no movement along the shore which was becoming more hazy as he sped away from it.

Now, as relief began to thaw his mind and body, he had to sit down abruptly on the seat behind the wheel, feeling his legs go rubbery under him. His whole body was shivering violently and he had to grit his teeth to keep them from chattering. The knuckles of his left hand were white where he gripped the wheel, so he let go and worked the fingers to loosen them.

'Holy shit!' he whispered. This was serious! These guys were not going to let up on him. Back in Athlone, he had thought that it would be only a matter of time before the two men grew tired and went back to Dublin. Now he knew it was not like that. They were much smarter and more determined than he had given them credit for. They had guessed that he was on Jacky's boat, and they knew that, out in the loneliness of the lake, their job would be easier.

They had hired or stolen this cruiser and followed him. With a shudder he realised that if they had wanted him so badly before, how much more they would be determined to get their hands on him now. He looked back again towards the markers at the entrance to the river, but there was still no sign of a boat or movement along that distant shore.

Donny pushed aside his fear now and forced himself to think. He would have to get off the lake, and the sooner the better. And it would have to be along the east shore, which, he noticed, had begun to slope away to form a wide bay on his right. He swung the wheel over and began to search the rush-lined shore for any inlet which might turn out to be a wharf or a harbour. But there was nothing. Every gap in the wall of reeds showed only the dark shapes of low rocks by the shore.

Donny picked up a pair of binoculars from the shelf beside him and scanned the shoreline directly ahead. A dark shape on the water's surface flitted past his vision. He swung the glasses back, focusing. Two buoys, a black and a red, took shape near the neck of what seemed to be a large, wooded peninsula protruding into the lake slightly to the north-east of him. Here, surely, was the harbour that he sought.

He had just pushed the wheel over to bring his craft onto a new course when he suddenly remembered the packet. His first reaction was to duck his head into the cabin doorway and scan the worktop and table. Clear! What if Slits or Dogs had it in their pockets? It would be too much to hope for. He eased back the throttle abruptly and the craft wallowed in the water. He had to be sure.

'Please, God!' he prayed, as he stepped down into the cabin. 'Please let them have it!' He stepped gingerly over the glass that was scattered over the floor and began to search the drawers on the right of the sink unit. His suspense did not last for long. There, in the very top drawer, its dull plastic staring obscenely up at him, lay the packet.

'Shit!' he groaned aloud. 'Shit! Shit! Shit!' He slammed the drawer shut again, as if by doing so he could contain the potent evil that lurked there, and hurried back to the helm. Anxiously he scanned the bright waters behind him, but there was no other craft in sight. He pushed the throttle hard forward, felt the nose of the craft lift as the churning propeller bit, and aimed once again for the neck of that distant peninsula.

At that moment, however, an object far over to his left caught his eye. It was another cruiser. It had just emerged from behind a group of scattered islands and was heading in almost the same direction as he was. He studied it through the glasses. The name, 'Sealegs,' was printed in bold, red lettering near the prow. Then his heart gave a great, thumping leap. Something was flapping from the rail at the stern of this craft. He steadied the glasses against the rolling of the floor under him. Jeans! His jeans! His stomach seemed to do a somersault. It was Jacky's boat! Here was a friend! Help was at hand! With rising excitement, Donny swung the wheel over and put Firefly onto a new course that would take it behind the other craft. Jacky had said that there was a harbour on the mainland near Rabbit Island. Now all he had to do was follow the other craft and it would take him there.

A short while later, Donny had settled his craft into the frothy wake that flattened out the waves behind Sealegs. Eagerly he kept watch through the swaying binoculars, but the only sign of life on board the other craft was the craggy outline of a large man at the helm. Jacky must be below deck in her cabin. He wondered what she was thinking. Was she disappointed? Was she sitting there, glumly wondering why he had left so suddenly, without a word, without a message? She could never have suspected the truth. And what a surprise she would get. With delicious anticipation Donny imagined the look on her face when she would see him stepping out of Firefly, the rush of questions bursting to be asked.

But even as Donny savoured the scene in his mind, the rugged outlines of Jacky's dad moved again into his vision and reality returned with a bump. He knew then the script would have to be changed. He couldn't just step out of Firefly and introduce himself to Jacky's dad, although he had to concede that there might be a certain, grim humour in it which Flagon and Swamp would appreciate.

'Hi, I'm Donny . . . friend of Jacky's . . . out for a spin just to keep those two jerks from gettin' the heroin . . . Oh, that? Just a bullet hole . . . but it's only a small one . . . Pardon? Oh, just last night . . . 'sa matter of fact, I spent the night in her cabin . . .'

'Cut!' Donny's mind screamed at him. This wouldn't do. There must be another way.

He spent the next few minutes trying to invent a plausible story which he might use on Jacky's dad, but he gave up then. Any story he could concoct would be even more far-fetched than the truth, and that was pretty crazy. No, the best thing to do would be to wait until Jacky and the adults had berthed and gone into the house on Rabbit Island. Then he would land on the island, sneak up to the house and, when a suitable occasion arrived, he would give Jacky the beck. He had a slight uneasy feeling that Boloney would consider this plot to be 'a little thin', if he were to produce it in an English assignment, but he consoled himself with a vague optimism that something would work out.

The craft ahead of him was, by this time, ploughing directly towards the twin markers which Donny had seen earlier. He now realised that the wooded prominence which he had taken to be a peninsula was, in fact, an island — almost certainly Rabbit Island. He studied it closely through the binoculars but could see no building of any kind in the dense wall of foliage that shimmered in the thin afternoon sunlight.

Ten minutes later, Sealegs veered inwards towards a stone wharf on the lee side of the island. Donny eased back the throttle and cruised slowly past, wondering if he could attract Jacky's attention. He gyrated in lazy circles while the visitors were received by a couple who emerged from the shrubbery at the end of the wharf, and he watched anxiously as the adults disappeared into the shrubbery again in the direction of a white-walled, slate-roofed house, half-hidden in the towering firs. Jacky stayed on the wharf, however, a lonely figure looking out across the lake.

She didn't notice Firefly's approach until it was within fifty yards of her. When she looked up, her face was serious and she watched impassively as it approached the wharf. Donny pulled back the lever and Firefly's nose dropped. It seemed to flounder for a moment in its own turbulence, before pushing slowly forward into the berth behind Sealegs. When Donny stepped out from the shadowy canopy, holding the stern rope, Jacky was standing at the end of the wharf, looking morosely down into the peaty water below her.

'Excuse me, miss,' said Donny coolly. 'Could I have me pants back now please?'

She started. 'Donny!' Lightning flashed across her face when she looked at him. Then she was beside him, holding his hand in an impetuous gesture of delight.

'What happened?' she asked, gazing in wonder from him to the boat. 'I thought you were gone . . . out to the road.' She shook his hand urgently, her excitement spilling all over him. 'What happened?' she insisted. 'Tell me!'

Donny told her his story: how the men had taken him by surprise and how he had outwitted them. She was agog with admiration and anxiety when he recounted the final struggle with Slits.

'Wow! They're really serious!' she exclaimed when he had finished. Then she saw the wound on his head. 'Oh, you hurt your head!'

He felt the lump on his head gingerly.

'Yeh,' he said, 'that's another one I owe Slits.'

'Lets have a look,' she suggested. He bent his head and her fingers lightly examined the wound.

'Ooh! It's nasty, Donny,' she said. 'You'd better get it seen to.'

'I will,' he assured her, 'soon as I get home. Listen, I gotta go.' He looked for his gear on Sealegs' stern, but it was not there.

'Your clothes,' she said, reading his thoughts. 'They're gone to the house. I told them they were mine. But I'll get them for you. Won't be a minute.' She started towards the house.

'Hold on!' he said. 'Can you make a couple of phone calls for me?'

'Sure,' she replied. Donny gave her Bill's and Flagon's numbers.

'Just tell 'em where I am, and that I'm on my way home now.'

At that moment, Donny saw a tall, gangling figure emerge from the pathway behind Jacky, and approach them along the wharf. It was a youth, about the same age as Donny. Jacky saw the alarm in Donny's face and turned quickly.

'Geoffrey!' she exclaimed.

'Yes.' Geoffrey's cultured voice had a casual confidence about it. 'What in blazes is going on here?' He stared at Donny suspiciously through thick glasses, perched on a long, thin nose. His enlarged eyes surveyed the baggy trousers and soiled sweater that Donny was wearing. 'Where on earth did this fellow come from?' he asked, suspicion giving way to mild amusement.

'It's OK, Geoffrey,' Jacky said hurriedly, and Donny sensed the alarm in her voice. 'This is Donny, and he's a friend of mine.'

Geoffrey, sensing her defensiveness, pushed home his advantage.

'A friend?' Geoffrey's eyebrows shot up in disbelief. 'A friend!' he repeated with a well-bred snigger. 'Does your Dad know about him, Jacky? 'Cos if he doesn't I think your friend here is out of bounds.' He turned to Donny. 'This is a private mooring, you know. And hire boats,' he indicated Firefly, 'are not allowed to moor here without permission.' He stood in front of Donny, waiting for — indeed demanding — a response. Jacky was getting annoyed.

'For God's sake, Geoffrey!' she blazed. 'Will you stop being such a . . . a prig!' Donny thought it was time for him to intervene.

'I think you're a bit off-side yourself,' he said. 'Jacky's a friend of mine. I just called to have a chat with her and when I'm finished my conversation with her I'll leave. OK?'

But Geoffrey was glowing with confidence. He raised his head to look down on Donny through the lower half of his lenses.

'I'm afraid it's *not* OK,' he insisted. 'Certainly not until my parents and my cousin's father have been made aware of . . . what's going on here. If you are what you claim to be, sir, then you won't mind accompanying us to the house, where we can verify your credentials.'

Donny smiled. He hadn't heard such a mouthful of verbiage in a while, not even from Bill Moloney when he was well warmed up. Geoffrey was taller than he, but not as heavy, and Donny had sensed a certain adolescent awkwardness in his lanky frame.

Geoffrey now stepped to the edge of the wharf and held out his hand imperiously as a sign that Donny and Jacky were to lead the way while he would bring up the rear. Jacky, her eyes aflame with anger, stomped her food on the stones and gathered herself for a blistering attack, but Donny forestalled her.

'Don't do this, Geoffrey,' he said quietly. Geoffrey was about to insist, but he saw something in Donny's eyes which caused him to change tack.

'It seems that I shall just have to go and ask them to come here,' he said, turning to walk away.

'Geoffrey,' Donny called. Geoffrey stopped. 'Geoffrey, can you swim?'

Geoffrey closed his mouth suddenly, a puzzled frown on his face.

'Of course I can swim,' he replied with indignant suspicion. 'Why?'

Donny moved like lightning. Geoffrey took a step backwards, his right arm coming up defensively, but Donny was quicker. He grabbed the outstretched arm and, with a deft twist of his body, sent Geoffrey hurtling over the edge of the wharf. The look of shocked surprise on Geoffrey's face was swallowed by the swirling splash as he went under. Donny turned back to Jacky.

'Jacky, I'm sorry. But there was nothing else I could do.'

She was staring at him, still startled by the suddenness of his move. Then her face crumpled and she doubled over with laughter. Beneath them, Geoffrey was huffing and puffing as he surfaced and began to stroke for the wharf side, his glasses gripped in his right hand.

'You bastard!' he shouted.

'I'd better go,' Donny said to Jacky. 'You can send on the gear . . .'

'No, Donny. Listen!' she spoke quietly, so that Geoffrey, now clutching at the wharf stones, could not hear. 'Take your boat round behind the island. There's a little wooden jetty there. Wait for me. I'll not be long. Go on!'

Geoffrey had got a foothold in the stonework and his long, bony hand grabbed the edge of the wharf near Donny's foot. Jacky was already untying the stern rope. Donny felt in his pocket for the keys.

'You'll pay for this! You . . . you punk!' Geoffrey said to Donny's feet. The avenging angel hauled himself out onto the wharf and stood up. Lake water leaked out of him onto the dry stones. But Donny was already in the cockpit, pushing in the key and starting the engine. He looked out to see where Geoffrey was and when he saw him he switched off the engine again. Geoffrey, a look of fury on his face, was coming towards the cockpit. Donny stepped back out onto the wharf to meet him. He didn't really want to fight, but he had to, he wanted it to be on open ground. Geoffrey halted several feet from him.

'You're going to be sorry for this!' he blustered. Suddenly Jacky thrust herself in the space between them.

'No, Geoffrey. Don't,' she pleaded. 'You're only making things worse.'

'Leave him alone, Jacky,' Donny said. 'Just keep out of it.' But it was too late. Geoffrey now felt doubly anxious to retrieve his honour. Suddenly he pushed Jacky violently to one side and rushed at Donny. Donny twisted to ward off a vicious kick. Then he lunged forward. His shoulder caught Geoffrey under the right arm and sent him staggering backwards. The momentum carried Geoffrey to the very edge of the wharf. He teetered. Donny, following up, tried to grab him, but Geoffrey slapped his hand away, Then, too late, he tried to catch Donny's hand. As if in slow motion, Geoffrey keeled over, arms flailing the air, and plunged straight down.

'You rotten bast . . .!' Splantch!

Donny didn't wait for him to surface. 'Get back to the house quick!' he told Jacky, 'before he gets out.'

'OK, but wait for me,' she warned. She was already moving away. Donny freed the bow rope, leaped into the cockpit, started the engine and reversed towards open water. When he looked back towards the island, a dripping Geoffrey was pacing along the end of the wharf, gesturing at him to come back and fight.

9

Donny had some misgivings about heading out into the lake again, even if only as far as a jetty somewhere along the shore of the island. By staying on the lake, he knew he was exposing himself to a danger which he sensed was lurking somewhere along the low shore towards the south west. He wanted to be ashore and into the safety of the countryside. More immediately, he was concerned about the storm which Geoffrey would undoubtedly create when he arrived, wet and humiliated, at the house where the adults were. He could imagine the inquisition which Jacky would have to undergo then. Who was this 'punk'? Where had she met him? What was he doing on a cruiser, dressed in ridiculous clothes? Donny shuddered. He hoped that Geoffrey hadn't recognised the pants and sweater he was wearing. The more he imagined the cross-examination, the more he felt certain that it would be impossible for Jacky to get away and meet him.

Now, suddenly, an even worse fear struck him. He had been dimly aware for a while that there was something important that he should have remembered, but it had refused to surface. Now it came, and it gripped him in a clamp of dread. It was the last shouted phrase that Slits had flung at him as he scrambled to his feet in the swaying dinghy, holding his head: '. . . sister is dead . . .'

'Christ!' Donny whispered. Maeve! Surely they wouldn't touch her. His fear almost made him swing Firefly round on the water and head for the mainland. But he didn't do it.

'Ten minutes!' he told himself. He would wait for ten minutes at the jetty, if he could find it. Then he would go. He couldn't wait any longer.

Now as he cruised slowly westwards along the south shore of the island he became aware that the wind had freshened and the lake was becoming rougher. A rhythmic thumping sound came from the prow as it pushed into the waves and occasional showers of spray splattered over the windscreen and the canopy over his head. A dark bank of cloud jutted above the low hills on the far western shore of the lake. A little nearer, a white cruiser was drifting slowly northwards. Otherwise the lake was empty.

Donny found the jetty hidden behind a rocky outcrop which protected it from the waves. He aimed Firefly at a little beach to the left of the jetty and, knocking it out of gear, let the waves drift it in. A quick burst of acceleration in reverse slowed it for long enough to allow him to leap onto the timbers, the stern rope in his hand. In a moment Firefly was securely tied.

Donny found the waiting almost unbearable. He paced tensely back and forth along the small jetty, his senses alert to any sign of danger. The white cruiser he had seen earlier was almost out of sight now, but another one had appeared from where he thought the mouth of the river should be. It too seemed to be heading north, but he watched it anxiously for any change in course. He had switched off Firefly's engine and now strained his ears for any sound that might come above the swash of waves on the rocky shore and the sough of wind in the tall trees.

Six minutes passed and the inactivity became too much for him. He realised that Firefly was in a poor position to make a quick get-away, if that should be necessary, so he untied the ropes, pushed the stern away from the jetty and, as the craft drifted parallel to shore, he hauled the nose forward until it faced outwards towards open water. He tied the ropes loosely again and resumed his pacing up and down.

When fifteen minutes had passed, Donny decided he would have to go. First, however, he would have a quick look inland, so he stepped down off the jetty and entered the green tunnel of foliage through which the path led upwards onto the island. Come *on*, Jacky, he thought. He would be glad to be back in his own clothes. When the ground levelled out, he found himself on a widening path which led to a circular clearing, surrounded on all sides by a dense hazel thicket in which there were several narrow openings. He stopped, listening. He heard only the wind and the muffled waves. Then, somewhere away to his right, he heard the shrill alarm cry of a blackbird.

'Hi, Donny.' The voice made him jump. Jacky was coming towards him under an arching hazel to his left.

'Jeez!' said Donny. 'You scared the . . .' She came towards him, smiling. She now wore a brown leather jacket over a white sweater, and faded jeans pushed into high, leather boots. In one hand she held his denim gear and on her back was slung a small, red haversack.

'Ah! You got the gear. Great!' he said, taking it from her. 'I was hopin' I wouldn't have to head back in this stuff.' He indicated the clothes which, now drying, were beginning to hang loosely on him again.

'No,' she said, her laugh almost nervous. 'That gear of Dad's is a real switch-off.'

Donny felt that he couldn't just turn and go.

'How's Geoffrey?' he asked lamely.

'Very clean,' she laughed, 'and not very happy. Oh, but he was furious! And the language he used!'

'Did he rat . . . I mean, did he tell the others?'

'Yes, the rotten sod! I tried to get him to say that he'd fallen in the lake by accident, but that only made him worse. The *names* he called you! And such a *story* he told — most of it bloody fiction!' Her eyes flashed with anger. 'Dad sent me to my room when I wouldn't tell where I met you. And Geoffrey! He made you out to be some sort of sex maniac.' Her eyes grew serious now. 'He said there was something in the paper . . .'

'What? In the newspaper? About who?' Donny was alarmed now.

'About you, Donny. 'Least I think it was you.'

'Me!' he demanded. 'It couldn't be! What'd it say?' He could see that she didn't want to say it.

'Geoffrey said something about a man found near a station in Dublin. He'd been beaten up . . .'

'Go on!' he ordered.

'The police wanted to talk to the man's wife and her brother.' She paused, watching him intently.

'Go on!' he repeated defensively. 'What else?'

'Something about an assault on a teacher — and drugs.' She laughed nervously.

Donny stared in disbelief. How could this have been in the paper? What were Maeve and Bill Moloney doing? How could they let the paper write a story like that?

'Listen,' he said. 'I told you about that stuff — how it really happened. Did you get a chance to ring Bill or Flagon?'

'No. I never had a chance. Geoffrey kicked up such a row.'

Donny made up his mind to go now. 'Listen, Jacky. I've gotta go. I have to get back to town. Which way should I go when I get back to land?'

She didn't answer. Her eyes told him that something was bothering her still. He caught her by the shoulders. 'Jacky,' he said firmly. 'It isn't true — what the papers said — I mean, the way they said it. It didn't happen like that. I told you the truth. That's it.' It was important to him that she believe him now. She searched his face for a moment and then the cloud cleared.

'I believe you, Donny,' she said simply. 'Let's go.'

'What do you mean, "Let's go"?' he queried. 'You're not comin'.'

Her face was already set. 'I am. I'm coming with you,' she announced firmly.

'Wait a minute. Hold on. You can't!'

'I can!' she retorted. 'And I am! I'm not staying round this rotten dump any longer.' Sensing his growing resistance, she hurried on. 'Look. I told you about school, didn't I? I said I'd rather run away than go back. Well, they're sending me back — Dad and that silly floozie, Veronica! He told me so himself, before he sent me to my room. So I'm going!' Donny opened his mouth to speak but she went on. 'Anyway, I'm not really running away. I'm just going home. Dublin's where I live, remember? I'll ring them when I get there. That's all.' She shrugged her shoulders as if it were the simplest thing in the world.

Donny felt he should be dominant and firm, but he couldn't do it. He turned away from her, looking back along the path that led to the jetty, not sure of what he wanted. When he turned back to her she was swinging a set of small keys playfully in front of her face.

'We have a way of travelling,' she laughed.

'What?'

'A bike — a motorbike. It belongs to Uncle Dan, but he doesn't use it any more. Only Geoffrey. It's in the boathouse on the far side, in the cove. I stole the key.'

Donny's mouth opened a little wider. He knew it was crazy.

'Listen, Jacky,' he said, as calmly as he could. 'I'm already down for assaultin' a teacher, probably beatin' up the brother-in-law, pushin' drugs, stowin' away on a boat, an' you want to add stealin' a bike an' . . . an' kidnappin' to the lot. Jacky, it's just not . . .'

'Donny, I'm going anyway,' she said decisively, 'even if you don't take me with you. But we'd better hurry. They were going to ring the police back at the house.'

Donny didn't protest further. 'C'mon,' he said, and turned towards the jetty.

'Oh no, you won't!' An imperious voice behind them jolted them to a standstill. Donny turned. It was Geoffrey. He was standing framed in a gap in the hazels, glaring belligerently at them through his thick glasses. With a start, Donny realised that Geoffrey was holding a rifle in his hands and that it was aimed at a point not very far above Donny's head.

'Geoffrey,' Jacky began, but she was cut short.

'Thought you'd escaped, hadn't you?' he sneered at Donny. 'Well, you haven't, have you? You just weren't smart enough!'

Donny pushed past Jacky. 'Hold it! Stop right there!' Geoffrey commanded, his voice rising in pitch, and he lowered the barrel of the gun slightly. Donny stopped.

'Geoffrey, have you gone completely mad?' demanded Jacky, trying to get past Donny's restraining hand.

'Mad! Me?' Geoffrey scoffed, brandishing the gun in what he considered to be a more threatening manner, and taking a step backwards at the same time. 'The only one around here who appears to have gone completely insane is you, Jacky. I *saw* you sneaking out of the house. I *knew* what you were up to.' His face became more serious, more severe. 'Jacky, have you any *idea* who this fellow is? He's the one that's in the paper, for God's sake! He's the drug pusher they're looking for in Dublin! Have you no *idea* what you're getting yourself . . .'

Donny spoke, his voice calm, despite his annoyance. 'Geoffrey, don't point that thing at us if it's loaded. It could go off.' He gestured with his hand as if to wave the barrel to one side. Geoffrey took another step backwards.

'I'll use it!' he blustered. 'It's loaded — and I'll use it.'

Donny sensed Geoffrey's rising panic. He took another step forward.

'Put the gun down, Geoffrey,' he said quietly. 'You don't know the full story.'

'Just shut up, you!' Geoffrey shouted, jabbing the barrel towards Donny's face. 'Stay back! And shut up! The police will be here in a minute. You can tell it to them!'

Donny saw a large, moss-covered boulder protruding from the path behind Geoffrey.

'OK, OK, I'll talk to them. There's no need for the gun. Just put it down, before someone gets shot.' He made another deliberate step forward.

Geoffrey stepped back quickly. His left heel struck the rock and he lost his balance. The barrel of the gun went up. He put his left hand out to grab a thin hazel branch but, before he could recover, Donny was on him. Donny grabbed the rifle barrel and forced it upwards, aware of Jacky's cry as he twisted it away. Desperation and blind fear gave Geoffrey strength. Squealing horribly, he held on doggedly to the gun as Donny twisted it over and back. Geoffrey's glasses slipped off one ear and dangled across his face.

'Let go!' Donny ground through his teeth, but Geoffrey held on, struggling to get to his feet. In exasperation, Donny drew back his right foot and slammed it into Geoffrey's groin. With an agonised yell, Geoffrey released the gun, clutched himself and rolled over on the ground, groaning and gasping.

'I'm sorry, Geoffrey,' Donny panted. 'But you shouldn't have done this!' He held the rifle gingerly in his hands, stepped away from the prostrate Geoffrey and examined it closely. He knew vaguely how it worked. He pulled back the bolt and a shiny .22 shell flipped out and fell on the ground. He spotted another shell just below the empty chamber, so he searched for a release button and, on finding it, he unclipped the narrow, black magazine from the weapon.

'You could have killed one of us with this, you berk!' he growled at Geoffrey, as he pocketed the fallen shell and magazine. 'Now you can go look for it.' He turned and swung the rifle in a high arc over the nearest hazel thicket. Geoffrey, now on his knees searching for his fallen glasses, looked up momentarily to follow its flight and listen to its crashing descent.

Donny glanced at Jacky. She had come nearer and was now glaring angrily down at her vanquished cousin.

'Geoffrey, I know you probably wouldn't believe us, even if we told you the truth. So we won't try. I'll explain it to you some other time! All I can say is that you've behaved like an . . . an ignorant wally! So goodbye. We're going now, and you can tell them what you like!' She stepped firmly in Donny's direction. 'Let's go!' she said. Geoffrey got to his feet, still holding his groin, fixing his glasses on his nose.

'You'll be sorry!' he croaked, his little eyes fixed on Jacky. 'You're making a terrible mistake! Do you not realise who he *is*?' He pointed a loose finger in Donny's direction. Donny turned back towards him. He was beginning to feel annoyed again.

'Shut up, Geoffrey!' he threatened. Geoffrey retreated in haste along the path.

'He's a drug pusher, Jacky!' he shouted. 'A pervert! How can you go with him? He'll . . . He'll probably *rape* you!' He stopped short to focus again on his target, but when he saw Donny coming for him, he turned and sprinted madly out of sight behind the bushes. Satisfied that his fake attack had worked, Donny turned back towards the lake.

'C'mon,' he said.

Geoffrey's cracked voice floated to them over the hazels. 'He's a sex maniac, Jacky. Don't go with him!'

Grimly, Donny untied the stern rope, coiled it quickly and flung it on board Firefly. While Jacky cast off the bow rope, he started the engine. Then, when she had stepped aboard and pushed off, he aimed Firefly around the rocky outcrop and into the waves. Jacky came to stand beside him at the helm.

'Don't mind him, Donny,' she said. 'He's just . . . upset.'

'It's OK,' he said, but he was tired and hungry and his feelings were confused. 'One thing you can be sure of, though. He's gone leggin' it back to the house now, an' the shit's really goin' to hit the fan any minute.' He pushed the throttle forward as far as it would go and the cruiser responded, nose in the air. 'Are you sure it's safe to go back this way?' His anxiety to be off the lake was now more acute than ever.

Jacky glanced at his face, sensing his unease.

'Yes,' she said emphatically. 'Just swing left a little more and aim for that tall tree to the left of the marker. That's where the harbour is. It'll only take a few minutes. We'll be all right then.'

'I hope so,' Donny grumbled, his voice raised above the thumping of waves against the hull.

Anxiously, they watched the stone wharf where Sealegs was moored, but it remained deserted as they motored past. Soon Donny was nosing Firefly into the calm waters of the mainland harbour. Hurriedly they tied the ropes to the metal rings, all the while watching the wharf on the island with apprehension.

'Right! Let's go!' urged Donny. Then, remembering his clothes, he leaped aboard the craft again, ducked down into the cockpit and picked them up from the floor where he had thrown them. He would put them on later.

He was about to rush out again when he remembered the packet. He hesitated, then reluctantly stepped down into the cabin, took it quickly from the drawer and stuffed it into the pocket of his pants.

When he leaped down onto the stone paving of the harbour wall, he noticed that Jacky was watching the island intently.

'Look,' she said.

In the distance, Donny saw a figure running onto the wharf beside Sealegs. He recognised Geoffrey immediately. As they watched, another figure appeared beside the first and, towering over him, stood looking intently towards the harbour where Donny and Jacky were. It was Jacky's dad. Donny's eyes were drawn irresistibly to her face but, as he looked, her expression darkened and set.

'I'm not going back!' she stated firmly. Donny was aware that her voice had become husky, but, as if she wanted to avoid his gaze, she abruptly turned away and walked purposefully towards a dense clump of laurels, behind which a low, shed-like building was half hidden. Donny cast a troubled glance towards the distant figures on the wharf and turned to follow her. He had troubles enough of his own, he told himself.

When Jacky reached the wide, double doors of the shed and began to insert a key in the lock, Donny realised what her intention was. He hurried to her side.

'Listen, Jacky,' he began. 'I'm not sure about this . . .'

'What's the matter?' she retorted. 'Can't you ride a motorbike?' Her abruptness took him aback.

'Yeh, I can. But it's not that. It might be better . . .'

'Don't worry,' she insisted, wrestling with the dull, metal bolt. 'We're only borrowing it. Remember? It belongs to my family.'

The resisting bolt shot back and the door creaked open. It was dark inside. As he entered, Donny saw a long sliver of light coming from low underneath two big double doors which gave access to the waters of the lake at the other end of the shed. In the dim light, he discerned two concrete ledges running along both sides of a sunken pit where a lake boat floated on black water. On the left hand ledge stood a motor bike, facing him.

'This is it,' Jacky said. Donny stared. It was big . . . and old, a miracle of polished chrome and lacquer and pedals. A film of dust lay on the long, leather seat and on the humped fuel tank which had the word 'Norton' written in old-fashioned letters along its side.

'Jay! A Norton 850!' whispered Donny. 'Swift! But it's ancient. It wouldn't start.'

'It will,' she insisted. 'Geoffrey uses it to go to Athlone. Try it.'

She handed him the keys. Donny hesitated, but when the memory of Slits' words on the lake came back to him, he made the decision.

'OK. If it starts, we'll take it.' He took the keys and stepped over to the bike. It was much bigger than Liam's old Honda, and Donny had to crouch on either side of it, studying the various levers and pedals before he felt confident enough to swing his leg over the broad saddle. He found the ignition switch and inserted the key. He opened the fuel tap and then, to familiarise himself with the controls, he worked each one in turn: the clutch and front brake levers, the throttle, and the gear and brake pedals at his feet. Unsure of the position of neutral on the gear pedal, he took the precaution of leaving the bike up on its stand while starting it. Now he opened the throttle a little and, standing up on the kick starter, he drove downwards with all his strength. The bike throbbed healthily beneath him and the exhaust pipe coughed smoke, but it did not start. He opened the throttle a little more and kicked down again. This time the motor roared into life. He gave it plenty of throttle and, while the exhaust clouds swirled around him, he checked the position of neutral again by watching the elevated back wheel. Satisfied, he pushed the heavy bike down off its stand and out through the open doorway, balancing his dry clothes on the saddle.

'Here. Put these on,' Jacky shouted above the noise. She held two old helmets and a pair of gauntlets. He put on a helmet and the gauntlets, resting the petrol tank against his knee. Through an opening in the bushes he saw that Sealegs had pulled away from the wharf on the island and was now ploughing towards them at speed. He straddled the bike and got set. When Jacky had her helmet fastened, she climbed on behind him. He felt the pressure of her hands on his waist. He handed his bundle of clothes back to her and she jammed them down between them.

'Ready?' he called.

'Ready,' she answered.

'Hold on!' he shouted. He clicked the gear lever down and let out the clutch. The bike shot forward in a surge of power. Jacky's hands suddenly grabbed him tighter as the bike careered across the little lane that led away from the lake. Donny wrestled the handlebars over as the front wheel mounted the low, thorn-crested bank. They wobbled, straightened, and then they were powering up between high, over-hanging hedges. Donny pushed up through the gears, leaning slightly at the corners, getting the feel of it.

'Right at the crossroads!' Jacky yelled in his ear. He slowed as the junction came, then swung right onto a wider, tarmac road, past a sign that said, 'Athlone 4km.' Donny opened the throttle, pushing the needle on the speedometer past sixty, and held it there. The road was a grey blur.

They had only gone a mile or so along the road, when Donny began to slow down. Seeing the sign for a petrol station on the left hand side, he turned into the forecourt. He didn't stop at the pumps, but eased the bike along the side of the low, white building, where a large, ungainly shrub would give it some cover.

'Hop off,' he called over his shoulder, and he felt Jacky dismounting. He got off, hauled the bike up on its stand and took off his helmet.

'What's up? Why are we stopping?' Jacky enquired.

'We're going the wrong way,' he stated. 'We'll have to get a map.'

'But this is the road for Athlone,' Jacky protested.

'I know,' he went on. 'But lookit what we're doin'! Goin' straight into the town! You know who we're likely to meet on this bleedin' road?' Realisation was beginning to show on her face.

'The cops,' she stated.

'Yeh,' he agreed, 'an' if Geoffrey has anything to do with it, it'll be the bleedin' army an' all.' He went to the corner of the building to watch for traffic on the road.

'They won't catch us, Donny,' Jacky reassured him. 'They don't know how we're travelling.'

'Not for a while, they won't. But what d'you think'll happen when they come across and find the bike gone? Red alert, that's what.' He was beginning to regret taking the bike. It would make them too conspicuous, and Dublin was a long way away. Now he turned to Jacky, her face, slightly pale, framed in the old helmet.

'Do you know any back roads around here?' he asked. She shook her head.

'No. All I know is that this one goes to Athlone.'

'We'll have to ask, or get a map,' he decided.

'Fair enough then. Let's try here,' Jacky suggested. She jerked her thumb at the building beside them.

They rounded the corner and entered the little shop. There was nobody behind the cluttered counter.

'Jeez! I'm ravenous, too!' Donny said, spying the bars of chocolate on the shelf behind. He slapped his pockets. They were empty apart from the packet. 'Shit! I left the shillings on your dad's boat.'

'That's OK, I've got it,' she reassured him. 'And lots more as well. I'll get you some.'

Just then a tall, thin youth in green overalls came in from the forecourt where he had been serving petrol. He provided them with a map and with a plastic bag containing provisions: coke, chocolate, biscuits and apples. Jacky paid while Donny began to savage an apple.

'Hang on,' he mumbled. 'Maybe the bike needs petrol.' He turned towards the door and then stopped suddenly. An unintelligible sound came from him. Jacky turned and followed his eyes to the forecourt. A silver-coloured BMW had just pulled into the pumps. Feeling the hairs rise along the base of his neck, Donny turned quickly away. His face was ashen.

'Quick!' he hissed. 'Say nothing, an' follow me. It's them — Slits an' Dogs!' He quickly put his helmet on, while the tall youth glanced at them curiously as he passed. 'Right!' Donny whispered. 'Walk slowly!'

He opened the door and went out, turning left around the corner to where the bike was. 'Hold these!' He handed the bag of provisions to Jacky, eased the bike down off its stand and manoeuvred it until it faced outwards again. He turned on the ignition. Through the leafless branches of the bush he saw the two men get out of the car and he felt the fear in his stomach again. He saw Slits speak to the attendant, who pointed towards the other side of the building. Then the two men disappeared from sight, leaving the car.

'Get on!' he urged Jacky swinging his leg over the saddle. As he plunged the kickstarter, he felt her hands on his waist. He eased the bike out from the shelter of the bush. The forecourt was deserted. He glanced into the shop. It, too was empty. They're gone to the jacks, he thought. And then, for about twenty seconds, Donny went crazy.

'Show us a can of coke!' he told Jacky. She started to reply but he cut her short. 'Quick, just pass one of the cans!' she took one from the bag. 'No. Hold it for a second!' he changed his mind. He swung the bike in a tight circle until it was alongside the BMW but facing in the opposite direction. 'Right!' he said and grabbed the can from her hand. There was still no sign of Slits and Dogs. Ignoring the youth, who had just returned the nozzle to its holder on the petrol pump, Donny gripped the can and, with one swift move, he swung it hard at the windscreen of the car. He felt the shock through his gauntleted hand, saw the sudden frosty shatter, dropped the dented can and gunned the bike hard out of the station and onto the road, heading for

Athlone. Awkwardly he pushed the bike up through the gears, not daring to take his eye off the road or look back. Rounding a sharp right-hand bend, he spotted a by-road approaching on the left. At the last moment he slowed and swung the bike onto the narrow road, then twisted the grip of the accelerator up hard again. The gears clicked under his foot and the bike went faster. The hedges along the side were now a blur.

Suddenly the road rose sharply ahead of him. Donny braked hard, but too late. The bike hit the rise and rose into the air. Donny had a split second to adjust before they landed on the other side of a humped bridge. There was a jarring shock as the suspension took the brunt. Donny wrestled with the handlebars, aware that the bike was still upright, aware of Jacky's shout and of her tightened grip on his waist. The bike slewed to the left. Donny made a frantic adjustment, squeezing the brake lever with all his strength. The machine swerved to the right and, just when he thought he had it under control, the front wheel mounted the edge of the raised bank along the roadside. The bike twisted sideways and Donny and Jacky were flung into the mass of vegetation on the inside of the bank. Donny braced himself for the crashing impact. He landed head first in a tangle of briars, felt the shock in his shoulders and then a sharp pain in his thigh. Frantically he struggled upright in the clawing, scratching briars, thinking only of Jacky. He heard her cry out and, turning, he saw that she, too, lay in the briars behind him. All he could see were her feet.

'Jacky!' he cried, plunging towards where she lay. 'Jacky! Are you all right?' He trampled and beat down the briars with his feet and gloved hands until he was beside her. She gasped with pain.

'Oh God! Jacky! Are you OK?' He bent down, caught her under the armpits and lifted her upright.

'Ooh! My side!' she groaned, bending forward to ease the pain.

'I'm sorry, Jacky,' he blurted out. 'I was going too fast. It was all my fault!' Helplessly he stood there, watching her grimacing, terrified that she might be badly hurt. She held his hand for support.

'Help . . . help me out of this,' she said. Together they struggled up onto the road.

'I think I'm OK,' she said after a moment. 'It's just my side. I landed on something hard.' She sat down on the bank holding her left side. 'Just give me a sec.'

The pain in Donny's thigh was getting worse. He eased himself down gingerly onto the grass beside Jacky. When he looked, there was a tear in his pants and blood was beginning to soak through the fabric around it.

'Shit!' Donny said.

Jacky stood up now, pain replaced by urgency in her face. 'Donny, we mustn't stay here. If those men come . . .' She glanced over the bridge. The road was deserted.

'Yeh,' he replied. 'But are you all right?'

'Yes. I'm OK. But I think one of the men saw us as we were leaving. He came round the corner. What did you want to break their window for? Now they know we're around and they've seen the bike!'

Donny had never felt so stupid in his life. This wasn't a game they were playing. Why had he let his anger make him act like such a denser?

Jacky strode over to where the bike lay on its side on the road, its front wheel still spinning, its rear wheel resting on the bank. Grimacing, she hauled it upright. 'Come on, you big twit, and drive this thing for me,' she called, grinning over at him. Donny walked over to the bike. Jacky gave him a friendly punch in the ribs and held the bike while he sat astride it. It started with the first kick.

'Let's go,' he said. The road behind was still empty. She climbed gingerly on and they started once again.

Donny drove more slowly now, turning and twisting through a maze of little roads that wound eastwards along the sides of the many drumlin-like hills. For the first few miles he anxiously watched the rear-view mirror for any sign of pursuit, but there was none. He felt strange. His arms and legs were very cold, and soon he noticed that his whole body was beginning to tremble violently. He knew then that he would have to stop.

A short time later, the wide entrance to a forest plantation appeared on the right of the road. Donny guided the bike between the two upright poles left as an entry for pedestrians and drove it over the rough track until they were out of sight of the road. They dismounted. With an effort, Donny hauled the bike onto its stand. Then his legs went funny under him and he had to sit down on a moss-covered rock beside him.

'Jeez!' he said. 'I'm feelin' funny.' Jacky put down the plastic shopping bag and Donny's bundle of clothes.

'Oh! Your leg! Look at it!' she exclaimed. 'It's pouring blood!'

It was true. The tear in his jeans was now the centre of a widening bloody stain.

'You're hurt, Donny,' she said. 'We'll have to do something with that.'

'Doesn't feel great,' he admitted sheepishly. 'Don't suppose you're a First Aid expert or anything?'

'As it happens, yes!' she answered. 'Let's have a look.'

Donny didn't want to have to take his pants off, so instead he gripped both sides of the rent in his pants and tore a long opening in them. Jacky wiped the blood away with her hanky and they examined the gash. It was short but deep and the blood was still oozing from it.

'We'll have to bandage it to stop the bleeding,' Jacky decided. She unslung the haversack from her back, took out a white T-shirt and tried to tear it along a seam.

'Here. Can you do this?' she asked. He took it and tore it into two pieces. Jacky cleaned the blood from around the wound and then deftly tied the strips of fabric around his thigh. 'You'll probably need stitches, you know,' she told him.

Donny leaned back against the rock. He was really annoyed with himself.

'Ah, God!' he exclaimed. 'I'm a stupid, stupid bastard!' She glanced at him in surprise. 'What a stupid, wally-head thing to do!' he went on remorsefully.

'Look, it's over now, Donny. It was an accident.'

'No. I was drivin' much too fast. I could have got us killed. It's just . . .' He shook his head in annoyance. 'I mean, I don't know what got into me . . . When I saw the car . . . an' those two bastards, I lost the head completely.'

'Donny, don't . . .'

'No,' he insisted. 'We could have sailed out of there no bother. They would never have noticed us. But I had to go an' be a nerd.'

She looked down at him and he saw that her eyes were bright with amusement.

'Well . . . it was silly, in one way,' she agreed. 'But, in another way, it was great! I suppose we were lucky they didn't follow us up that road.'

'Lucky we weren't bleedin' killed,' he said ruefully. But his anger with himself had been softened by her good humour. 'But you,' he remembered. 'You're hurt too. How are *you*?'

She patted her side gingerly. 'It's just a graze, I think.'

Donny was about to say, 'Giz a look,' but he stopped himself. He was now acutely aware that she was a girl and that you couldn't just look at a girl as you would if it were Flagon or Swamp. She unbuttoned her jacket and pulled up her blouse to examine her injury. In the smooth skin beneath her left breast, an ugly weal had begun to glow.

'How does it look?' she asked, with a laugh. 'I can't see it very well.' Donny's attention was momentarily focused on her bra and the curved fullness of her breast, and he felt himself colouring with embarrassment.

'It looks . . . OK,' he stammered. 'Eh . . . what I mean is you'll probably have a bruise.'

'Ah, who cares,' she said flippantly, as she fixed her blouse back in place.

Donny watched her face, trying to read what she was feeling. It suddenly occurred to him that she might already have had enough of this adventure. Maybe she was just keeping a brave face.

'Listen. If you want to . . . if you'd prefer to go back . . .' he faltered. 'I mean it's not working out very well.' He stood up, afraid of what she might say.

'No, Donny, don't say that,' she said. 'It'll work out fine. You'll see. All we have to do is get to Dublin. Everything will be OK then.' Impulsively she caught his arm and shook it to make him raise his eyes to her face. 'Come on. Let's have something to eat. We'll feel better then.'

Her face, framed in the old helmet, was close to his now, and when he looked into her bright eyes, a great rush of warmth seemed to wash over him. As she lifted off her helmet, he would have loved to lean over and kiss her on the lips, but was afraid of being too pushy. Instead, he punched her delicately on the chin with his gauntleted fist. 'OK,' he said. 'Let's bring on the grub!'

They ate chocolate and fruit, sitting on a bed of pine needles under a tall spruce. Overhead, the clouds were breaking and the mid-afternoon sun was pouring through the gaps.

'Donny?' Jacky said thoughtfully, through a mouthful of apple, 'have you any other family, besides Maeve?'

'There's a couple of aunts and cousins. But Maeve's the only one close.'

'What about your parents?'

'They're both dead,' he replied impassively, surprised that his feelings were dormant.

'Oh. I'm sorry, Donny. I didn't realise . . .'

'It's OK,' he said. ' 'S funny. I remember Dad fine, 'cos I was twelve when he died. But my mum died when I was only three, an' yet I sometimes feel as if I know her, although I can't remember her. It's hard to explain. Sometimes it just feels as if she's around . . . you know.'

'You mean, close to you, even though she's dead?' said Jacky, slightly awed.

'Yeh. Something like that,' he said. She was quiet for a moment.

'My mum's in England,' she said then, answering the question that he was struggling to phrase in his mind. 'She went over to live with Gran when she and Dad had a . . . a disagreement.' More cheerfully. 'I'm going to visit her in summer.'

Donny tried to be kind. 'Will she be back?' But the question sounded blunt.

'I don't know.' She sighed. 'I'd like if she did. I'd like if things were the same as before. But sometimes I think they never will.'

'I know what you mean,' Donny said. The wind ghosted mournfully through the tall spruce above them. Then the thought of Maeve came crashing back into his mind and Donny jumped up. 'C'mon, let's go. We'll have to find a telephone. I want to make a few calls.'

'OK,' she replied, 'and it would do no harm to find out where we are. Then we can use the map.'

'Right. We'll ask the first person we meet,' he promised.

They were back on the road only a few minutes, when they came upon an old man pushing a bike up a long hill. He looked at them sedately and said, 'If ye keep on about three mile, ye'll come to Horseleap.'

'That's on the main Dublin road,' Jacky said to Donny. 'I know the way from there.'

10

The village of Horseleap nestled in a bowl made by a ring of low hills. Donny parked the bike in a gateway about fifty yards from the main road and they walked to the junction. The Dublin road was alive with cars and trucks speeding past. A short distance along it they saw a telephone kiosk.

'No. Too exposed,' Jacky decided. 'We could be spotted by any passing car. Let's try the pub.'

The public phone in the small pub was located at the end of a nearly empty bar. Jacky took some change from her haversack. Donny first rang Bill Moloney's number. He let the phone ring for a long while, but there was no reply. He shook his head grimly.

'I'll try Flagon.' Flagon's mother answered the phone.

'Donny! David's been wondering about you.' She was the only person Donny knew that didn't call her son 'Flagon'. 'Hold on, I'll get him.' There was a pause; then Flagon's voice.

'Don! Where the hell are you? What's goin' down?'

'It's a long story, Flag. I can only give you the bones.' Donny briefly told Flagon how he had been forced to jump onto the Athlone train, and how Slits and Dogs had followed him. 'It's unbelievable, Flag. They caught up with me this morning but I gave them the slip. I'm OK now . . .' Flagon whistled in appreciation at the other end. 'I'm in a place called Horseleap now. Should be home in an hour or two. But I'm a bit worried about Maeve. I rang Bill last night an' asked him to drop over to see her, but I'm not sure if he did. Would you ever give her a shout, or him, if there's no one in the gaff.'

'Amn't I bleedin' hoarse givin' him a shout, Don. Me'n Swamp called four times today already, an' there's no reply. The same with your gaff, Don. What the hell's goin' on?' A feeling of dread grew inside Donny.

'Hold on, Flag. Are you sure Maeve's not there? She could have been out shopping.'

'Positive, Don. Me'n Swamp've been beatin' a path to the door all day, since we saw the bit in the paper. But there's nobody there.'

'Christ!' said Donny.

'What is it, Don? What's goin' on?'

'I think Slits' mob have got Maeve, and maybe Bill and Moira too.'

'But why would they pull a stunt like that?'

'Because they want me, Flag. Or what I've got belonging to them.' The last few coins were running out. 'Listen, Flag. Will you be at home later?'

'All evening, Don.'

'OK, stay put. We'll be there in a couple of hours.'

'Right, Don. Who've you got with you?'

'Oh, it's just . . . It's a friend, Flag. We'll see you soon. Cheers.' He put down the phone and turned to Jacky.

'You heard that?' he asked. She nodded, her face grave. He grabbed the helmet and gloves from the counter beside him, but she put a restraining hand on his arm.

'Donny?'

'Yeh?'

'Donny, I think it's time to go to the police.' He turned back to look at her, a frown creasing his forehead.

'The cops?' He thought about it.

'Yes, Donny. It's getting . . . serious now.' She squeezed his arm. 'What do you think?' He sat down on the high stool by the phone. He was feeling shaky again.

After a few moments he said, 'Yeh, I know they're supposed to deal with stuff like this. But what'll happen if I go to them now? I'll end up in the slammer. It'll be the Jaws thing all over again. 'Thing is, you see, if I'm right about that mob getting Maeve an' the others, there'll be no-one to speak for me . . . except Liam, an' that bastard's not likely to tell the cops that he was deliverin' a load of heroin or stuff. He's more likely to shove it all onto me to save his own hide.' He felt in his pocket for the packet and took it out. He squeezed the plastic and his thumb left a depression in the contents. 'The bastard! He's been nothing but trouble ever since she met him! Just couldn't keep his sticky fingers away from this stuff!'

'Do you know what's in it, Donny?' He shook his head.

'Well, it isn't sugar anyway . . . No. It's probably heroin or cocaine. Those guys are into this stuff. The only thing is, as long as we have this, we're holding some kind of a hand.'

'But what'll we *do*, Donny?'

'I think,' he said after a pause, 'I think we'll head for town an' see Flag first, before we do anything else. OK?'

She hesitated. 'All right, Donny.' He rose to go, but her hand held him again. 'Donny, hang on a sec. I need to make a call too.'

'Sure,' he said, checking himself. He wanted to be away.

'I just want to tell him I'm OK,' she said. 'That's all. Then we'll go.'

Donny moved away while she spoke briefly to someone on the phone. She seemed subdued when she came back to him.

'Well?' he asked. She shrugged her shoulders.

'He wasn't there . . . He's gone looking for me . . . for us. I told Veronica to give him the message, when he gets back.'

'Did you tell her where we are?' She shook her head. 'Right. Let's go.'

Back at the bike, the first thing Donny did was to change back into his own gear in the shelter of the gateway. He kept on the sweater which Jacky had given him the previous night, as a protection against the wind when they would be travelling. From the tattered, blood-stained trousers he took the magazine from Geoffrey's rifle and the sinister packet and stuffed them in the pocket of his jacket. With difficulty he worked his jeans up over his injured thigh, grimacing with the pain of it.

'Right,' he said, tossing the discarded trousers over the gate beside him. 'Let's have a look at the map.'

Jacky, who all this while had stood silent and unmoving beside the bike looking down the street, did not respond. Glancing at her, he caught her wiping her cheek with the back of her hand.

'Hey,' he said, going over to her. 'What's up?'

She didn't try to hide her tears.

'It's nothing. I'll be all right in a minute.' She tried to brush the annoying tears away. 'It's just . . . everything.'

'What? Did Veronica say something?'

'No. It's not her. It's Dad. Things just aren't working out for him. He's making all the wrong decisions. And now this.'

Ah, shit! thought Donny, suddenly exasperated. As if he didn't have enough problems, now here she was turning on the tears. He might have known it would turn out like this, he told himself bitterly. Yet she looked so lonely. Despite himself, he made a half-hearted move with his hands and then, to his surprise, she leaned against him and he felt her head nestling under his chin. Impulsively he put his arms around her and held her, as if to protect her from the racking sobs that shook her body. Behind him, on the main road, the traffic growled and rumbled. A young boy saun-tered up the street licking the remains of an ice-cream. He stood for a moment looking at the motionless couple. Then he lost interest and moved on.

Donny was aware of a sudden lump in his throat and he found himself swallowing hard and blinking back his own tears. It was a long moment before he could speak.

'We're both up to our tonsils in it, aren't we?' he said hoarsely to the top of Jacky's head. He felt her answering nod and her arms tightening around his waist. 'But we won't be down-hearted, right?' he heard himself say. 'We'll go on fighting. OK?'

She looked up at him now. Her eyes were still wet, but she managed a weak smile. 'OK, at least we'll go down fighting,' she whispered.

Awkwardly he let her go and began to busy himself with the map, not sure how to deal with the strange, new excitement which he felt. It was courage and trust and affection and happiness and anxiety all rolled into one. He felt ashamed of himself for being exasperated with Jacky.

'Right. I think we should keep away from the main roads and the big towns. They'll be watching those. Let's try to find a quieter route home.'

He spread the map on the saddle of the bike and, together, they plotted a winding route through a network of by-roads that lay south of the main road. Jacky folded the map in such a way that their route could be clearly visible and tucked it inside her jacket.

'Right, Mr Pilot,' she commanded. 'Straight across there, and head for Clara!'

Back on the bike, Donny focused his attention on his driving. He was now more accustomed to the size of the bike and the workings of the controls, and he kept the speedometer needle above fifty as much as possible. Jacky gripped him around the waist, and the feel of her arms around him almost made him forget the trouble he was in. He was very glad now that she had come with him, and, although he mentally chided himself for even considering that he might be falling in love, he had to admit that he was having fun and that just being with her made him feel good. How it was all going to end, he didn't know, but he decided that he would worry about that when the time came.

The route they followed now was through a rabbit-warren of little roads that wound between low, hazel-crested drumlins and long, winding eskers. When in doubt they would stop at a crossroads or junction, dismount and study the map. Once, they pulled into a petrol station and Jacky bought two gallons of petrol. Then they were on their way again, always keeping a wary eye for danger.

The sun shone continuously from the southwest now, but, although the air felt warm whenever they stopped, Donny grew colder and colder on the bike. The wind seemed icy at the neck of his shirt and the bottoms of his jeans. His thigh felt brittle and throbbed dully whenever he moved his leg, and at the back of his head he felt an insistent ache. His eyes were tired from squinting against the wind and the tiny insects of the road. He wished he were home.

At last they came down a steep, leafy by-road, dipped into a hollow and saw a sign that made Donny slow to a halt on the roadside. It read, 'Dual carriageway ahead.' They dismounted and took off their helmets.

'Jeez!' exclaimed Donny. 'I'm perishin'.' He rubbed his hands together and began to pace along the road to warm himself, but he had to stop because of the pain in his leg. Now that the engine was switched off the silence seemed loud, but in a moment they began to hear the hiss and growl of traffic over the slight rise ahead of them.

'If we are where I think we are,' said Jacky, who had already spread the map on the bike seat, 'we've only six or seven miles to go. Look, this is where we are.' She pointed to a place called Rathcoole on the map. Donny, looking over her shoulder, agreed.

'Yeh. Good! Flag'll be wonderin' what's keepin' me.' She glanced at him quickly.

'What do you mean "me"? Am I not invited too?'

'Yeh. 'Course you are,' he protested, 'if you want to . . . I just thought you'd want to get home straight away.'

It took her a moment to decide. 'I'll go with you. I'd like to meet Flagon. And anyway, we have to make sure that Maeve is OK. I can go then.'

Donny was pleased. 'That's cool. You'll like Flag. He's doss.' Then a thought struck him. 'But what about the bike? Maybe we'd better leave . . .'

She shook her head. 'No, we still need it. When it's over we'll leave it back.'

'OK, let's go.'

Several minutes later, they were out on the wide dual carriageway, at speed. Donny kept the bike in the fast lane, pushing it into the spaces as they appeared in front of him until the needle was steady at seventy-five. The power of the engine under him and the nearness to home were restoring his confidence. Maybe everything would be all right. Maybe his fears were groundless.

They turned right onto the Long Mile Road and, at the far end, the lights were red. Donny reluctantly slowed to a halt. Only a few hundred yards, he told himself, and they would be into the side streets, into the familiar maze of alleyways and parks and red-brick houses. Jacky's left hand tapped urgently at his side. Out of the corner of his eye, in the lane to his right, Donny saw a big, dark-blue car coming to a stop. Even before he saw the large lettering along its side, he knew it was a Garda car. He steeled himself, glancing back at the lights. Still red. When the door beside him began to open, he panicked. There was a momentary gap in the cross traffic. He gunned the motor and let out the clutch hard. The bike jerked forward with a squeal of rubber, shot across in front of a blaring truck and into the fast lane. They passed three cars on the outside, before an oncoming bus forced Donny to pull in. In the mirror he saw the flashing light and he knew the police were after them. 'Get off the street!' his mind screamed at him. He knew there was an alleyway on the right, just before the petrol station. He slowed, waited an interminable second for an on-coming car to pass, then slewed the bike across the street and into the pot-holed lane. The bike bucked and leaped beneath them. Donny held his breath, aware of Jacky's arms tight around his waist. With a bit of luck they would reach the T-junction before the Garda car would reach the mouth of the lane. But, just before he swung left, he spotted the flashing light in the mirror again. A sharp right turn immediately; then a left onto a wider street. Donny was on home ground now. He swept past a main right junction, raced another fifty yards and then turned into another narrow alleyway. When he saw the three concrete bollards across the far end, he knew they were safe. With relief, he squeezed the bike between two bollards and surged through the gateway and into the park. The narrow path, bordered by wide, well-groomed playing fields, led straight to the exit on the far side. Donny allowed himself a grim smile of satisfaction. By the time the police would have circled round, he and Jacky would be lost in the maze of houses that lay ahead.

11

Five minutes later, Donny turned the bike into the short driveway of a small, terraced house in Drimnagh. 'Will you open the gate?' he asked Jacky, indicating the wicket gate at the side of the house. He wheeled the bike round to the rear and hauled it up on its stand. The small enclosed garden with its well-kept lawn seemed unusually quiet after the throb of the engine.

Suddenly the back door of the house was flung open and Flagon, munching a mouthful of something, appeared.

'Don! How is it?' Then he saw the bike. 'Holy Cow! Where'd you get *that* thing!' His eyes widened in amazement, and he looked from the bike to Jacky and back to Donny. 'Did you . . . ? You didn't . . . !'

'We did, Flag,' Donny said. 'An' it's a long story. I'll tell it to you later. The main thing is, we're back. Oh, by the way, Jacky. This is Flag. I told you about him.' Jacky held her hand out across the bike and Flagon shook it awkwardly.

'Hope it wasn't all lies he told you,' he quipped.

'He told me all the bad things,' she replied, laughing. She liked him immediately.

Donny, his gloves and helmet off, shifted impatiently from foot to foot.

'Anyway,' said Flagon, sensing the urgency. 'Business before pleasure. Come in. You look like you could do with a cuppa.' He headed for the door. 'I think I've got something for you, Don.' They followed him into the small kitchen.

'What, Flag? What is it?'

'Well, today after you rang, me'n Swamp went nosin' around again — we're only just back — an' there's def'ney no-one in either of the two houses. Gone! Vanished!' He plugged the kettle into the wall socket and began to take slices of bread from a wrapped loaf, while Donny stared at him, wide-eyed.

'They couldn't have,' Donny said quietly. 'The bastards! They couldn't have taken them all!'

Flagon began to spread soft margarine on a slice of bread.

'I dunno, Don. But there's somethin' weird goin' on, I'm tellin' you!' He dug deep into a pot of jam with the point of his knife and heeled a lump of jam onto the bread. Abruptly he stopped and studied Donny evenly. 'I think you should call the cops, Don.'

'Call them!' Donny snorted. 'We've been bleedin' tryin' to keep away from them! They nearly got us over in Walkinstown! What good'll *they* do?'

Flagon pushed a plateful of bread and jam across the table in Jacky's direction and turned towards the steaming kettle, his brow creased with a frown.

Jacky spoke. 'Flagon's right, Donny. There's nothing we can do if they really *have* Maeve and the others. We don't even know where they might be.'

Donny scratched his head in frustration. 'Anyway, is that all you've got for me, Flag? Is there something else?'

Flagon dropped two tea bags into the teapot. 'I'm not sure, Don. It might be nothin'. It's just that I remembered seein' a strange car outside Boloney's place early this mornin' on the round. A silver-coloured Granada.' He shrugged his shoulders. 'Well, you know. No big deal. Coulda been anybody's. Coulda been Boloney's rich uncle up from the country. No,' he reflected, staring out through the window. 'She had Dublin plates. Couldn't a been from the country . . . Well, anyway, I just noticed it. An' what you're sayin' is that Boloney musta gone down last night an' brought Maeve up to his gaff, an' the mob followed them up. An' that's how they took them outta there this mornin'. 'Cause the car was gone when we went back.'

'Yeh! Great!' Donny said, disappointed. 'That part is easy to figure out. But they're gone. Could be anywhere by now. Did you even get the number?'

Flagon was indignant now. 'No, Don. But how was I to know there was somethin' up? But here, let me finish. It was buggin' me all evenin' since you rang that I'd seen that car before, somewhere on the round. I nearly dried me bleedin' brains out thinkin' about it.' He spread jam liberally on another slice of bread. 'An' then it came to me . . . only a few minutes ago when I was lyin' there.' He licked jam with relish from his finger. Donny stopped chewing and waited. Flagon waved the bread knife in a dramatic flourish and pointed it straight at Donny. 'Cork Street,' he announced. 'Yard in Cork Street, near the glass shop. Between that an' the . . .'

Donny pushed his chair back suddenly and stood up, trying to swallow a mouthful of bread. 'C'mon. Let's go!' He wiped the crumbs from his mouth and grabbed his helmet. 'Better give Swamp a shout. We might need him.'

Jacky stood up too, and Flagon caught her silent plea. He shrugged his shoulders.

'There's no harm in havin' a look,' he said. Donny, already on his way to the door, turned back to Jacky. 'Jacky, we're just going to have a look. If you don't . . .'

'I'm coming,' she declared, reaching for her helmet.

'OK, Flag,' said Donny. 'We'll head for Cork Street on the bike. You give Swamp a shout, an' follow us on as soon as you can. Is his bike still workin'?'

'Just about,' said Flagon, picking up the phone. 'Right, we'll be there in about fifteen minutes. Don't do anything until we get there. OK?'

'OK,' replied Donny, and he headed for the bike.

It took Donny and Jacky only five minutes to get to Cork Street. It was a long street, flanked by groups of old, terraced houses, occasional shops, high walls, high gates, warehouses and the trappings of decay. They passed the hospital on the right and cruised all the way to the end of the street, but there was no silver-coloured Granada in sight. They turned and came back through the busy traffic. Donny saw the glass shop which Flagon had mentioned. It was on his right, last in a row of low, red-brick houses. Beside it, a grey-walled warehouse loomed over the street. Its high, mesh-guarded windows were in darkness in the late evening sunlight, and the tall, brown gates which gave access to the inner yard were closed.

Donny pulled into the hospital car park and parked the bike behind a van. He felt very tired and his thigh was so painful that he had to lean back on the bike for support. Above him the wide, indifferent sky, tinted with red from the setting sun, stared down at him. He felt wretched.

'Is your leg bad? Jacky asked, her face showing her concern. 'There's a hospital right beside us. You could get it looked at.'

'Naw,' he replied with a wry smile. 'That's maternity. I don't think they'd be much good to me. Not for a while yet anyway.'

'No, I suppose not,' she agreed. 'But listen, if we don't find anything here, you'd better have it looked at. OK?'

He nodded, his face softening when he looked at her. 'I will.'

Silent, she stood beside him now, and watched the traffic moving past. He stole a glance at her face, wondering what she was thinking. She caught him looking at her. 'What? What is it, Donny?' she enquired, slightly self-conscious now.

He looked down at his hands. 'Nothin',' he said quickly. 'Well . . . not nothin' . . . I was just wonderin' . . .'

'Wondering what?'

'Why you're doin' this, I mean, you don't have to. You didn't have to come with me to Flag's place, or down here, or even the bike an' everything.'

'Oh, that's simple,' she said with a careless laugh. 'I'm running away from home, aren't I? Remember?'

' 'Course I do. But, with all the trouble I'm in, you know. It's *dangerous*! If Slits an' Dogs had caught us . . . They could *still* catch us . . . An' the cops . . . They can pin all kinds of stuff on me. An' if you're with me, you might get into trouble too.'

Impulsively, she caught his hand. 'They won't get us, Donny.'

'Maybe not,' he conceded. 'But I still don't . . .' She put her finger on his lips. 'I don't *really* know why I'm doing it,' she said, suddenly serious. 'I've never done anything like this before. It's just that I want to do it. It's a feeling. Don't you ever have feelings?'

'I do,' he heard himself say. Everything was out of focus except her face looking up into his, and he knew that he was going to kiss her. But, just as he bent his head, he was jolted back to reality by the squeal of bicycle brakes and the clatter of wheels over the rough tarmac beside them.

'Hi, Don,' Flagon called, slowing to a stop. Swamp, following close behind, but not being equipped with the same lightning reflexes, bounced past, hauling vigorously on his brake levers. His back wheel skidded to the right. Swamp put his left foot down, hopped on it four times in quick succession and then sat down abruptly on the tarmac, letting go of the bike. It came to a halt several feet from him. Swamp levered himself onto his feet, all the while clutching the two bulging pockets of his jacket. He swung a friendly kick in the general direction of the bike and turned to greet his friends.

'Bleedin' machines!' he muttered. 'Oh, hiya, Don. Good to see you. Heard you were playin' hide an' seek with Maguire an' his mob . . .' He stopped when he saw the motorbike, his eyes bulging. 'Holy Shiners! A Norton! A real, live Norton!' He briefly inspected the machine and then turned his gaze, still full of admiration, on Jacky. 'Is it yours?'

'Well, not quite,' replied Jacky, clearly amused by the arrival of Swamp. 'It belongs to my uncle. We've just borrowed it for a while.' Swamp's face signalled the fact that he would love a spin on the machine, but his good sense told him that there were more serious matters in hand.

'Well, Don. What've we got here? D'you think Maeve an' the others are here?' he asked. Donny suddenly felt very tired. Swamp's joking was irritating.

'How the hell do I know? We'll have to look first, won't we?'

'Sorry, Don. No need to bare the fangs,' he said warily. Then, in an effort to smooth the troubled waters, he rummaged in the pockets of his jacket and pulled out two walkie-talkies. 'I brought these along, just in case we might need them.'

Donny's irritation increased. He knew, however, that Swamp had read nearly all of the Hardy Boys books when he was thirteen, so he made allowances.

'Here. Give me one of them,' ordered Flagon, an excited gleam in his eye. 'I'm goin' to have a dekko.' He made to take one of the radios, but Donny intervened.

'No, Flag. You don't need one of them. Just go along an' have a look, like a good chap, an' come back an' tell us. That's all.'

Shrugging his shoulders in disappointment, Flagon swung his leg over his bike and pedalled furiously away down the street towards the gates. The others watched him park the bike against the kerb and saunter carelessly towards the gates. When he came to them, he stopped, looked theatrically in both directions, stepped closer, and tried to peer through the gap in the centre where the gates met.

'Christopher!' exclaimed Swamp. 'We might as well send a telegram to let them know we're coming. Look at what he's doin' *now*!' Flagon had suddenly dropped on all fours in front of the gate, and was squinting underneath it with one eye. He was on his feet and sprinting in an instant. He leaped onto the bike, shot across through the traffic and headed towards them at full speed.

'He musta spotted something!' whispered Swamp.

Even before he skidded to a halt beside them, they knew he had news. His eyes shone like beacons on a dark night.

'It's there! The Granada's there!' he exclaimed excitedly.

'Oh, yeah!' cried Swamp. 'Let's go get them! C'mon, lads . . .' His voice trailed off when he saw Donny's face. Donny tried not to let his feelings sour his words.

'Look, fellas. We can't go in just like that,' he explained patiently. 'These guys mean business. Slits an' Dogs tried to *kill* me down on the lake.' The others, hearing the passion in his voice, looked at him, disbelief in their eyes. 'Yeh. They tried to bleedin' shoot me — that's what I said — with real bullets. You know, the little bits of lead that just drill into you an' then you go splat against the ground.' He nodded his head in the face of his friends' astonishment. 'An' for all we know, Slits an' Dogs are already back an' waitin' right inside those gates for the Light Brigade to come chargin' through.' He let it sink in for a moment.

'You mean, they actually . . .' began Swamp.

'Shot a real gun at you?' finished Flagon. Jacky's sober face told them that Donny was telling the truth.

'Wait a minute!' said Jacky. 'Look!' She was pointing down the street towards the gates. A tall, thin figure had just emerged from them and was now looking carefully up and down the street. Donny recognised the long, ginger hair immediately.

'Don't all stare together,' he said quietly, 'but that's your man that hangs around with Slits. You know him, what's-his-face.'

'McCann,' breathed Flagon. 'I'd know him anywhere. Watch him.'

McCann now turned back to the gates and appeared to close them. Then he walked along the footpath, away from the watching group. He crossed to the right hand side and vanished into a shop.

'He's gone into the chipper,' said Swamp. Donny watched the distant chip shop with growing interest.

'Let's jump him,' said Swamp impulsively. Flagon turned on him.

'Woh? You?' he scoffed. 'That fella is just out of the slammer. And d'you know what he was in for? Stabbing' a bloke nearly to death with a knife, that's what!'

Swamp puffed out his tubby chest indignantly and pushed his glasses farther up along his nose. 'Least if I sat on him, he wouldn't get up,' he sniffed.

Indecision ran like wildfire through them. Then Donny made up his mind.

'Gimme one of those. Quick!' He held out his hand for a walkie-talkie. Swamp handed it over. 'The bike, Flag!'

Flagon leaned his bike towards Donny, his face mirroring Swamp's puzzlement. Donny lifted his stiff leg over the saddle.

'I'll contact you if I get in,' he said. Flagon snapped out of his bewilderment,

'Wait a minute, Don.' But Donny had pushed out into the street and the rest of Flagon's protest was lost in the roar of a double-decker that thundered past. Donny dodged through the on-coming traffic to the white line in mid-street, freewheeled until a gap appeared to his left and then swerved across to the kerb. He skidded to a stop beside the high wall, leaned the bike against it and, with his eyes fixed on the door of the chipper, hobbled at speed to the high gates. The righthand gate yielded to his touch and opened a fraction. He took a deep breath and slipped through, trying to concoct the first line of a plausible story in case he might need it. The small yard was empty, however, except for the silver Granada.

His eyes swept quickly around. They took in the high wall to his left, the two-storied office-block facing him and the high metal door, slightly open, of the warehouse to his right. The two doors of the offices were shut and the windows, blanked out by blinds, showed no lights behind them. He moved towards the great metal door, his runners making no sound on the oil-stained concrete. He flattened himself against the wall, listening for a sound from within, but there was nothing. He inched his head round the door-jamb. Inside he saw piles of cardboard cartons, wooden packing cases, a forklift and cylindrical bales of black material scattered in apparent disarray on the warehouse floor. There was nobody in sight. His eyes shifted upwards to the high window of an odd two-storied structure that filled the far, right corner of the building. An electric light burned behind the window and, as he watched, a shadow passed slowly across it. A metal staircase ascended steeply to a door that opened inwards on the right of the window. So that's where they are, Donny thought.

The walkie-talkie in his hand came to life. He lifted it to his mouth, turning down the volume dial as he did so.

'Yeh, Swamp.'

'Don,' Swamp's voice sounded distant, metallic. 'McCann's on his way back with the grub. Watch it. Over.'

'OK, Swamp. If I'm not out in half an hour call the cops. Over and out.'

Donny acted fast. He first went to the gates and slid the heavy bolt home. This would keep McCann on the outside for a while. Then he padded quietly into the warehouse and examined the catch on the huge metal sliding door. Satisfied, he found a nook behind the cardboard cartons and waited, listening for sounds above the faint hum of evening traffic from the street outside.

Time had stretched taut before he heard the gates outside rattling. He tensed. They rattled again, this time louder. Then he heard knocking, a pause, more insistent knocking, and then the door at the top of the metal stairs opened and heavy steps resounded through the warehouse. Donny waited until a stocky figure had plodded out into the yard before he moved. Then he left down the walkie-talkie, tip-toed to the door, poised himself and pushed with all his might. The rollers above began to turn, slowly at first, then faster. With a thunderous clang, the door slid home and he slammed down the hasp that would keep it shut. Outside, he heard shouts, and then metallic tugging sounds.

Donny raced silently along the aisle between the cartons and took the steps three at a time, oblivious of the sudden stabbing pain in his thigh. When he burst into the small room, a swarthy man with a drooping black moustache was rising from a table in the centre of the floor. When he saw Donny, he lunged towards the worktop beside him. Donny saw the gun and dived for it too. His hand closed on the barrel just as the man's hand closed on his wrist. The man's other hand clawed at the handle of the gun, but Donny drove his right shoulder into the man's chest. Then he grabbed the gun with his two hands and whipped it in a swift arc over the man's head, twisting his arm and sending him staggering to his left. Before the man could recover, Donny caught him across the midriff with the full force of his left knee. The other grunted with pain, but he still held on to Donny's wrist. And now Donny felt the strength of the man, for he jerked Donny powerfully towards him, twisting downwards at the same time. Donny felt himself falling, but at the last split second he launched himself off his left foot straight at his adversary. His right shoulder caught him in the chest, knocking him backwards against the table. Unable to bear the weight, the table skidded across the floor, scattering chairs. It was then that Donny became aware of the figures lying on the floor in the corner.

He had only a fraction of a second to see them, because the floor came up to meet him and then he was rolling over and over among the upturned chairs, kicking and biting, desperately trying to keep his grip on the gun, but knowing also that he was weakening, that the other was stronger. He brought his leg up to block a second savage lunge of the man's knee, but he knew then that he was beaten.

Suddenly, out of nowhere, there was a solid 'thunk' and something hit the man's head from behind. His grip loosened momentarily. With a last desperate twist, Donny broke free, rolled over and scrambled to his feet. He held the gun at arm's length with his two hands, pointing it, finger on the trigger, now desperate enough to use the weapon in the face of another onslaught. But it never came, for, when he looked down, it was to see that Bill Moloney, despite being bound hand and foot, had somehow launched himself across the head and shoulders of his captor, who was now struggling to extricate himself from under Bill's considerable weight. When, after a brief struggle, he did manage to do it, he found himself staring into the round black hole at the end of the gun in Donny's hands. He looked once into Donny's eyes, and then his resistance collapsed.

'Don't! Jays, don't shoot!' he pleaded. His hands shot upwards and he skittered on his backside over to the far wall, his eyes white with terror. To his right Donny saw the frightened eyes of his sister, Maeve, her mouth taped over, her hands and feet bound. Beside her lay Moira, Bill's wife. But Donny wasn't ready to socialise yet; his attention returned to the man.

'Lie! On the ground! Face down! Now!' he said in what was intended to be a cool masterful tone, but the command came out as a strangled shout. The man flattened himself on the floor nevertheless. Donny searched the draining-board and sink and found a knife. He wiped the buttery blade on his jeans and began to saw at the ropes round Bill's wrists, holding the gun in his left hand. When the rope parted, he handed Bill the knife. Below them, in the warehouse, the metal door complained from the battering it was getting.

'Any of the others have guns, Bill?' Donny enquired urgently. Bill, in the process of peeling the tape from over his mouth, held up one finger, then raised one hand above the other to indicate tallness.

'The tall one?' Donny asked. Bill nodded and yanked the tape free.

'Christ! Donny! Are we glad to see you!' he exclaimed. He attacked the rope around his ankles with the knife. 'Are the police outside?'

'No. Not yet,' Donny replied. The noise from below was thunderous now and he knew that he'd have to go. 'Listen, Bill. Will you look after him? I gotta go.'

'It'll give me great pleasure,' replied Bill grimly, standing up. Donny sped down the steps. The slamming outside had stopped. Instead the men were calling.

'Hey! Macko!' one shouted. 'Wot's up? Open the bleedin' door!'

Donny raised the gun. He aimed first at head height and then about a foot above it. He closed his eyes and squeezed the trigger. A blast of sound and fire exploded from the barrel and he staggered back from the shock. A small, round hole had appeared magically in the metal door. He heard someone outside say, 'Jaysus!' and then there was silence. The radio on the floor crackled again and he picked it up.

'Donny! Donny!' It was Flagon's anxious voice. 'Are you OK? What's goin' on?'

'They're here, Flag. Maeve an' the others are here. But there's two guys outside. Can you see what they're doing?'

A pause. Then Flagon again, more urgently. 'They're gettin' into the car, Don!' Donny flung the radio onto the ground and launched himself at the metal door. His finger was bloodied when he at last forced the hasp up. He hauled at the door. It slid open and he darted through the gap. He saw McCann, his ginger hair streaming behind him, leap into the passenger seat and slam the door. The Granada shot forward towards the gate. Donny aimed for the side window behind the driver's head and squeezed the trigger again. Another explosion, the shattering of glass, the car swerving sideways, crunching into the gate pillar, dead stop, the two men shouting through the shattered window, 'OK! OK! Don't shoot!' all in a blurred instant of time. Then the wide-eyed, frightened faces of Flagon, Swamp and Jacky crept round the gate pillar, fearful of another shot.

'Get back!' Donny screamed at them, keeping the gun aimed at the two men still in the car. 'One of them has a gun!' He moved to the passenger door, standing a little behind it as he'd seen the cops do in the movies. 'You! Out!' he barked. The tall one sulkily stepped out. 'On the ground!' He hesitated for a moment, but when Donny lifted the barrel a fraction, he lowered himself to the ground. Donny swung the gun back towards the heavy-set man in the driver's seat. 'Now you!' he ordered, vaguely aware of the people standing outside the gateway, cautiously looking in. 'Over here!' he said to the heavy one, who was now standing on the far side of the car. He hesitated for a second, his eyes flickering from Donny to the gateway and back again. Donny aimed at a point several inches to the right of the man's left ear and blew a fistful of plaster off the wall behind him. The heavy one jumped around the back of the car and shuffled sideways over to stand beside his companion. He lowered himself sullenly onto his hands and knees, all the time watching Donny.

'Lower!' Donny croaked, suddenly aware that the gun was wobbling uncontrollably in his hand. He grabbed it with his second hand but it was no use; he was trembling all over. A strange feeling took root in his stomach and began to rise to his throat. The feeling was verging on panic when Bill Moloney came out of the warehouse. He took one look at Donny and then rushed over to him.

'You've done enough, Donny,' he said, taking the gun gently from his hands. 'Take a break. I'll deal with it now. Has someone called the police?' But Donny couldn't answer, because he saw Maeve coming for him with outstretched arms. He grabbed her and held her.

'Oh! Donny! Thank God you found us!' she sobbed. 'Thank God you're safe!' Over her shoulder, through a haze, Donny saw Jacky, Flagon and Swamp coming for him, their faces shining with delight and admiration.

'Ya *boy* ya!' exulted Flagon, and then they engulfed himself and Maeve in a boisterous embrace. Exhausted, Donny felt like crying and laughing all at the same time. Their exultation, however, was short-lived, because Bill Moloney, now standing over the two prostrate men, was calling.

'Will one of you boys please call the police,' he requested, 'in case no-one else has thought of doing it.' Donny extricated himself from the clinging arms.

'I'll do it, Mr Moloney,' he said. 'You stay here, Sis.'

The crowd outside the gate had now grown bigger and, seeing it, Donny felt annoyed by the curious stares. As he passed the Granada, its wing crumpled against the pillar, he realised that the engine was still running.

'Kill the engine, will you, Flag?' Donny said, and Flagon jumped to do it. It flashed through Donny's mind that there was something different about the way in which Flagon and Swamp now regarded him, but he couldn't interpret it so he shelved it for later. He pushed his way out through the huddled onlookers to the ordinariness of the street, intent on finding a phone. Jacky and Swamp were close behind.

'Hang on, Don,' said Swamp. 'You've done enough. I'll get on the blower to the cops. There's one at the hospital. You lot wait there.' And he trotted away from them along the footpath.

12

Out in the street, Donny tried to get his mind to function normally and to make sense of what was happening. It seemed to him that there was too much data, and that his system of processing it was overloaded. Jacky stood beside him, bright-eyed, but her joy was now tinged with concern for him. She caught his arm.

'It's over now, Donny,' she reminded him gently. 'It's all over. You were terrific!' He stared at her, trying to concentrate on her words. 'The police'll be here any second,' she went on. 'Then we can go home.'

Donny nodded to show that he understood her. 'OK,' he muttered, 'OK.' He looked up the street towards the hospital, searching for Swamp, and then he stiffened, as if rooted to the pavement. 'Oh, no!' he said, the words half-strangled in his throat.

'What is it?' she asked, following his gaze. About fifty yards away, a silver BMW with a broken windscreen was approaching them along the street.

'It's them! The bastards!' he ground through his teeth. She tried to turn him back but he looked at her as if he had never seen her before and broke away. 'The murdering bastards!' He moved towards the car, now only twenty yards from them. Then they saw the weasel eyes of Slits Magee staring at them through the shattered glass. In the same instant, the car lurched forward and, with a loud squeal of tyres, it took off down the street. Donny shook off Jacky's restraining grip.

'They're getting away!' he croaked hoarsely. Then he was running back towards the gateway. Flagon had just emerged from the crowd. 'Flag! Where's the keys?' Flagon stopped, startled.

'Of woh, Don?'

'The car! The Granada!'

'Left 'em in her, Don. What's up?'

Donny rushed past him and plunged into the crowd. He desperately jerked open the car door and bounced into the driver's seat. He had driven Liam's old Hillman several times in the Park and he tried to remember it now. The engine roared into life when he turned the key. He was aware of the rear right door being jerked open and of Flagon tumbling into the back seat.

'Reverse!' Donny told himself. He pulled the gear stick back and let out the clutch. The car jerked backwards. Flagon was shouting incoherently. Donny pushed the stick into first gear and the crowd scattered as he surged towards them. He saw Bill Moloney's startled face to his left but he did not stop. As he turned into the street, Jacky dashed across in front of him and he had to brake violently. She rushed round, pulled open the passenger door and jumped in.

'Come on, they went down here and then left,' she cried.

'The BMW, is it, Don?' yelled Flagon, no longer speechless.

'Yeh. It's Slits and Dogs!'

Donny fired the Granada into third gear. They swung left at the T-junction, bounced off the kerb and then turned immediately into the Coombe. The BMW was nowhere in sight. As they flashed past Meath Street, Jacky cried, 'Up there, Don!' Changing gear, Donny kept going and took the next left, which was parallel to Meath Street. He punched the horn at a cyclist who wobbled out in front of him and jammed on the brakes at the T-junction.

'Which way?' Donny cried in despair.

'Right,' said Flagon. 'Left,' said Jacky. He swung left away from the city centre. Far ahead of them, near Guinness's, the BMW was overtaking a truck.

'Watch him!' Donny shouted. He changed down to third again. The engine, revving to a high-pitched whine, complained. The lights went orange at the Watling Street junction. 'Hang on!' yelled Donny. They shot through. Flagon took his head in from outside the window to say, 'He's gone right for Heuston Station!' But when they turned into Steevens' Lane, there was no sign of their quarry.

'Must've gone left at Bow Lane,' Flagon called.

'OK,' said Donny. 'We'll go left at St John's Road. Might catch him at Military Road.' They screeched into St John's Road, ignoring the baying of an eighteen-wheeler that trundled towards them from the river.

'There he is!' all three shouted together. The BMW had just swung onto the street about fifty yards in front of them. Donny pushed the pedal to the floor.

They squeezed past a labouring Beetle, honked a Mini to one side and got a clear space between them and the BMW. When they swung into South Circular Road, they were close enough to see the frosted windscreen in front of Dogs, and Slits' head framed in the clear opening where the coke can had smashed into it. Into Conyngham Road they were almost bumper to bumper. Donny saw Slits glance into his rear-view mirror. Then his head jerked up and he looked again.

'Shit! He's seen us!' Donny said. A cloud of blue smoke shot suddenly from the BMW's exhaust and it swung abruptly in through the narrow gates of the Phoenix Park.

'G'wan! Get him, Don!' Flagon urged. An oncoming driver stuck his Audi to the road when he saw the Granada powering through. Cogs growled and snarled somewhere in the gearbox as Donny found third again and pushed the pedal to the floor.

'Jeez! He's fast!' said Donny. The BMW went straight through an intersection. A blue car, coming from the right, swerved wildly away, its back end swinging across the road in front of the Granada. Donny clawed at the wheel, first left, then right, but the road was not wide enough. The front wheels mounted the slight rise onto the grassy parkland. The rear end bucked into the air, landed and slewed sideways. Flagon shouted something. Donny, remembering the bumpers at the carnival, spun the wheel over. The tyres burned the sappy grass, gripped, scattered the roadside gravel and then they were surging up the hill after the BMW, now dipping out of sight on the crest.

'C'mon!' Donny yelled at the Granada.

'They're getting away!' Jacky cried.

'Put 'er on the floor, Don!' exhorted Flagon.

'It's there already!' retorted Donny, willing the car to go faster. When the road levelled out on the top of the hill, however, they knew they were losing the race. The BMW was already several hundred yards ahead, weaving along the narrow road, pulling away from them towards the dense stands of trees that flanked the road on either side. Beyond them, Donny knew, lay the main thoroughfare through the Park.

'If he gets to the main road,' he muttered grimly, 'he'll have the legs of us!'

Suddenly, the brake lights of the BMW flashed bright red.

'What's that?' Flagon said, leaning forward between the seats, squinting his eyes. Indistinct against the dark trunks of the trees, a grey wall was stretched across the road in front of the BMW.

'It's the deer!' Jacky exclaimed. 'They're crossing the road!'

'Jeez! We've got them!' breathed Donny.

The BMW was almost stopped now. Donny saw the deer on the road wash away from the car, but the grey line didn't break. And then the brake lights went out and the BMW swerved suddenly to the left and bounced onto the open grassland.

'He's goin' round them!' yelled Flagon. 'Cut him off, Don!'

'Jays! Flag! D'you want to drive it?' Donny retorted. The suspension thumped and rumbled beneath them as they bounced off the road and onto the grass. He worked the wheel to straighten the wriggling tail.

'Go on, Donny!' cried Jacky. 'We're gaining!'

'He's goin' to have to go round the trees!' Flagon said.

Too late, Slits realised that the herd was too close to the trees to allow him a passage back to the road. Now he turned the BMW to the left, skirting the trees, searching for the gap that Donny could see several hundred yards to the north. But he had lost a lot of speed. The BMW wobbled from side to side as it strained to get traction on the damp grass near the trees, while the Granada, though still over fifty yards away, was hurtling over the rough ground.

'Watch it, Donny!' Jacky yelled suddenly. 'He's opening a window! The gun!'

'Get down!' Donny yelled. Twenty yards to his right, he saw Dogs' glowering face framed in the half-open window. He was aiming a gun at the Granada. Donny swung the wheel hard right. There was a sharp crack, a spray of glass, and a round hole appeared in the windscreen above Jacky's head.

'You bastards!' yelled Donny. He straightened the wheel and braced himself.

'Hold on!' he shouted at the others. The nose of the Granada caught the BMW just behind the rear door. Donny took the shock through his hands. Next thing he knew, Flagon had catapulted forward onto the gear stick. He gasped with pain.

'C'mon, Flag!' Donny shouted. 'Get off the stick!' Flagon rolled to the left on top of Jacky, who was struggling up from the floor. The BMW slewed round but kept going. Donny turned hard left to avoid the trees and changed down. Above Flagon and Jacky's incoherent shouts he felt the power surging up from the engine again. He looked for the BMW and found it, twenty yards to his left, travelling in the same direction. He saw Slits' window come down and he knew that Dogs was trying to get another shot at him. The gap in the trees was dead ahead, only thirty yards away. Instinctively, Donny swung the Granada to the left. 'Stay down!' he screamed. 'He's taking another shot at us!' The Granada's left wing slammed against Slits' door. Inside the BMW there was a flash, but the sound of the shot was swallowed in the tumult of grinding wheels and metal. Donny glimpsed the gap between the trees and swung the wheel to the left again. Slits desperately clawed the wheel of the BMW but the Granada was too heavy. With a splintering crash, the BMW hit the outside tree head-on. Donny wrestled the Granada to a skidding halt on the rough ground between the trees.

'Jeez!' exclaimed Flagon, looking back. 'It's in bits!'

Donny started to get out, but Flagon grabbed his collar. 'Jeez, Don, look out. They're armed!' he reminded him.

'I've got to,' Donny said simply. 'I'll be OK. Just stay here.' He got out and studied the BMW, its nose fused with the tree-trunk. There was no movement inside it. 'Be careful, Don,' Flagon warned from the Granada. Donny limped back warily, keeping close to the trees on the right. He saw Dogs first. His head was slumped sideways against the half-opened window. He was unconscious or dead. Donny could see no movement through the crazy pattern of the shattered windscreen or through the dark hole where Slits' head should have been. He was only a few yards from the crumpled bonnet, when the driver's door began to swing open. Donny froze, ready to dash into the trees. Slits got out slowly. His hat was gone and a trickle of blood ran from above his left eye. The thin covering of long black hairs had parted to reveal his white crown. He held onto the door for a moment, looking around him in a dazed manner, wiping the blood from his eye with the sleeve of his coat. Then he saw Donny. His upper lip curled into a snarl of hatred and he started to come round the door. In the distance Donny heard the sirens blaring, coming closer. He braced himself. But Slits stopped, turned and pulled open the partly closed door again. Donny knew then that he was going for the gun. He sprinted forward. Slits saw him coming through the hole in the windscreen and he ducked out again, clipping the edge of the roof with the back of his head as he came out. Donny launched himself.

His feet slammed against the door as Slits jumped back. The sharp edge of the door struck Slits on the left shoulder and threw him against the side of the car.

'You little bastard!' he snarled. 'You bloody little bastard!' and he charged.

Donny had planned to dodge to the left at the last second, but when he pushed off his right leg, it crumpled under him. He was halfway to the ground when Slits' knee and shoulder caught him in the chest, knocking him backwards. As he fell, however, Donny grabbed the lapel of Slits' coat and hauled downwards. Slits overshot, but his bony knees raked Donny's chest and head as he landed heavily behind. A fierce pain shot through the wound in Donny's thigh, yet he scrambled to his feet. He turned just in time to see Slits' polished shoe coming for his groin. He twisted away. The sole glanced off his thigh. As it reached the top of its swing, he grabbed it and hoisted it high. Slits' other foot shot from under him. He seemed to be suspended in mid-air for a moment and then his back whacked against the turf, jolting the wind from his lungs. With a triumphant yell, Donny moved in. But Slits was too sharp — he bent his leg and kicked straight up. The hard leather heel caught Donny under the chin. His teeth jarred together and something in his head exploded with the shock. He tried to shake the stupor from his brain but found, to his surprise, that he was face down on the grass. His mind screamed at him to move, do something, but he couldn't remember why, and his body simply refused to stir. The sound of police sirens was spreading through the trees around. Donny thought cynically, 'Late again!' But now, as the haze in his brain cleared, he became aware of other sounds, closer at hand: urgent sounds, cries and grunts and gasps. He shook his head and looked up. The sounds came from a tall grotesque figure that was engaged in a crazy dance close to the door of the BMW. He saw Jacky beside it, pushing against the door to keep it closed. As Donny got unsteadily to his feet, there was a heaving groan and the weird figure split in two. The head and shoulders went hurtling across the bonnet of the car and rolled to the ground. When it bounced up, Donny saw that it was Flagon, having been pitched headlong from his perch on Slits' back. The life flooded back into Donny's limbs. He saw Slits advance on Jacky, her back against the door of the car, her eyes flashing.

'Get outta the way, you bitch!' Slits growled at her. He raised his hand.

Donny yelled savagely and flung himself forward. Slits hit Jacky once across the face, before Donny reached him. Donny's right arm encircled his neck, tightened, and twisted down and backwards. But Slits was like a cornered animal now, and his strength was frightening. Desperately, Donny strained, but he couldn't bring him down. 'C'mon, Flag!' he screamed. His strength was almost gone, when he felt something hit Slits in the midriff. He was aware of Flagon, head down, recoiling, and coming again with his head. It sank into Slits' stomach and Donny felt him weakening. 'Get him again, Flag!' he grunted. He gave one last muscle-snapping twist to his body and Slits staggered. Flagon's next charge put him down. Slits went under Donny and tried to roll. Then Flagon landed on Donny's back.

'We got him, Don!' he yelled. 'Hold on to him! Pull the head off the little bollox if he moves!' Donny, sandwiched between Flagon and Slits, tightened his grip on Slits' neck and, all of a sudden, Slits gave in. Donny felt the resistance drain out of him, but still he wouldn't relax his hold. The police sirens seemed to be just beyond the trees. Then Donny remembered the packet.

'Here, Flag. Get off me!' he growled. Flagon rolled to one side and Donny reached with his left hand and tugged the resisting packet out of his jacket pocket. Between Flagon's legs he could see Jacky at the car. He tossed the packet in her direction.

'In the car, Jacky. Quick!' he shouted. He saw Jacky pick up the packet and move towards the BMW and then the air was suddenly assaulted by the raucous braying of police sirens and the dull thumping of heavy tyres on the grass near his head. Flagon got up and began to dance jubilantly on the grass beside him, gesticulating and shouting. Donny saw Swamp tumbling out of one of the police cars, eyes bulging behind his thick lenses. Beneath him, Slits was roaring and clawing at the arm which Donny still kept clamped around his neck.

'You'll be sorry, O'Sullivan!' he snarled. 'We'll get you for this, you and that little bitch . . . Aaargh!' Donny cut him off with another quick twist of his arm.

'Stuff it, Magee!' he spat into Slits' ear. 'We haven't even started on you yet. Just let us know when you get out, and we'll finish it!'

Strong hands began to lift him up.

'All right, lad,' a gruff voice above him said. 'You can let him go. We'll take care of him now.' Donny released Slits and got to his feet. A tall man with a bushy moustache towered over him.

'Your name Donny O'Sullivan?' he asked.

'Yes,' replied Donny. He found that he was shaking all over.

'We'd like you to come with us. There's a few questions we'd like to ask you.' The voice sounded sympathetic, but Donny hesitated. Someone came and caught his left arm. He made to pull it away but checked himself when he saw it was Jacky. He turned to face her, ignoring the big detective. He saw the red mark across her temple.

'He hit you!' he said, anger surfacing through his weariness.

'That's nothing,' she said, squeezing his hand. 'I'm glad it's over.'

'Me too,' he said, huskily. He took her in his arms and held her, feeling her arms tight around him. His heart was too full for words.

The big detective started to speak again, but this time Donny wasn't listening, for his legs were suddenly refusing to hold him up.

'I think I'm going to . . .' he started. Jacky staggered under his weight.

'Help!' she called. Big hands grabbed Donny from behind. He found himself being lifted into the back of a police car. The trees, cars and people were slowly spinning round, so he closed his eyes. He heard Jacky nearby, talking insistently. '. . . horrible men tried to kill Donny . . . beat him up . . . shot at him . . . accident . . . bad gash in the leg . . .'

The big detective tried to get a word in. 'Well, we only want . . .'

'But, can't you see, he's exhausted. He needs to get to a doctor, or a hospital. He's in no condition to answer questions. He's completely worn out.'

The big detective tried again. 'Now, Miss . . .'

'*I'll* answer the questions. I was there all the time. *I'll* make a statement. *I'll* tell you everything you want to know.' The big detective paused.

'Would I be correct in saying that your name is Jacky Anderson?' he asked drily.

'It is,' she said.

'Hmm. I thought so. Well, young lady, we'll want to be talking to yourself as well. In the meantime, I think you're right about our friend here. He looks as if he could do with a bit of medical attention.'

13

Donny woke with a start. He had heard a strange ringing noise. He looked around and found, to his surprise, that he was in a bed in a large room. The ceiling was high and vaulted, but he couldn't see much of the walls because of the cream coloured curtains that hung from a chrome rail that went right round his bed. Somewhere in the distance, a phone was ringing. From outside the windows came the hum of city traffic.

Donny started to sit up, but his body protested. It felt as if it had been put through a mill. His right thigh hurt most and when he ran his hand gingerly down along it he discovered that it was swathed in bandages. His chin felt tender and his neck muscles hurt when he turned his head. He lay back, studying the faded ceiling as the memories flooded in. The lake took shape in his mind's eye; the water shimmered and glistened. He remembered the frantic escape from Slits and Dogs on the island and the dogged struggles of Geoffrey. He remembered the wild ride across the country on a big Norton, the mad dash through the city streets in a Granada and the desperate struggle with Slits in the Park, and he frowned in disbelief. Surely it was a dream. Surely it couldn't all have happened to him in two short days. But then the image of a blonde-haired, bright-eyed girl floated into his mind and he knew that she, at least, was real, that she had been with him through it all, and that her name was Jacky.

His daydream was interrupted by a movement of the curtains. A nurse, clad in a white uniform and cap and carrying a small tray of medicines, appeared.

'Hello,' she said, and Donny noticed her kindly grey eyes. 'So you finally woke up. How are you feeling?'

'I'm OK, I think. Where am I?' he croaked.

'You're in the Mater Hospital,' she replied with a smile. 'They brought you in last evening. You'd been in some sort of battle, by all accounts.'

He recalled the grey ceiling of the ambulance and Jacky and Flagon and Swamp's faces near him as it travelled.

'Where are the others?' he asked.

'Well, your sister's here. When she saw you were asleep, she went to visit someone else. But she'll be back soon.'

'Oh, great!' he said. The nurse was shaking capsules into her hand. 'Was anyone else in?'

'No, just the two boys and the girl that were here when I came on duty last night. I expect they're at home now, catching up on some sleep. They seemed pretty worn out, especially the little girl. She your sister, too?'

'No,' Donny replied. 'Just a friend.' The nurse held out two capsules and a glass of water towards him. 'What's wrong with me anyway?' he asked as he hauled his body upright.

'Nothing very serious. A few stitches in the head and in the thigh; a few bumps and bruises here and there. Otherwise, mostly nervous exhaustion. You've had a pretty gruelling time, it seems. But you'll be as right as rain after a good rest.'

Donny took the capsules and swallowed them down.

'So, I can get up and go home,' he concluded.

'Hold on. Not so fast,' she said. 'Dr Robinson wants to have a look at you first. She'll be around in a little while. So, in the meantime, just relax and rest.'

When the nurse had gone briskly about her business, Donny lay back and thought about it all again. He wished Maeve would come, or one of the others; he needed to talk about it, to get it into perspective.

Just then, the curtains moved again and Maeve came in.

'Hello, Donny,' she whispered.

'Hi, Sis. Am I glad to see you. How's it goin'?' He held out his hand for her to take. She kissed him on the brow. 'Great, Donny,' she said. 'How is it with you?' She seemed unusually cheerful.

'I'm OK,' he replied. 'They have me stuffed with drugs. The head feels funny.' He paused for a moment, a frown furrowing his brow. 'It's all really been happening, hasn't it? I mean, all that stuff about the train to Athlone an' bein' on a boat an' Slits an' Dogs an' all?' Maeve nodded seriously.

'It's all true, Don. You've really been in the wars. But thank God it's all over now. You did very well, little brother. You've become . . .' She hesitated, glancing towards the curtain behind her. 'Well, they told me not to get you too excited . . . but there was something in the paper about you.'

'Oh, no!' Donny exclaimed. 'I was hoping that was part of the nightmare . . . .'

'No, not the bit on Thursday's paper. It was in this morning's. You're a hero, Don.'

'Gerroff!'

'No. It's true. I have it here.' She searched in her bag and extracted the paper. 'There it is.' Donny held out his hand for it but she held it back. 'No. I'll read it for you.' She folded it and began to read. 'The headline says, "Schoolboy cracks drugs ring." The Gardai have seized a large quantity of cocaine as a result of the resourceful action of a schoolboy and his friends. Donny O'Sullivan, a sixteen-year-old student at St Brendan's, Drimnagh, whose sister and several family friends had been kidnapped by members of the gang, took on the gang leaders almost single-handedly. Despite the injuries which he sustained at their hands, O'Sullivan, with two friends, drove through the city in a high speed chase to prevent the suspects from escaping. The chase ended in dramatic circumstances in the Phoenix Park when the suspects' car was in collision with a tree, and the occupants were overpowered by the three young people, one of whom, it is believed, was a girl. A Garda spokesperson confirmed that a gun and a large quantity of cocaine were found at the scene. One of the men arrested is in hospital, suffering from concussion. Gardai say that charges will be laid against them today.'

Maeve laid down the paper and looked at Donny expectantly.

'Jeez!' he breathed. 'They didn't get half of it! If only they knew! There's loads more! They tried to kill me down on the lake, you know!'

'I know,' she replied, her face suddenly serious. 'They told me last night. All your friends were here last night, but you were asleep. It must have been dreadful for you. Liam was very upset when I told him about it . . .' She realised, too late, that she shouldn't have mentioned Liam's name.

'Where's Liam?' Donny demanded, recollection raising the anger in him again. 'How is he?'

'He's OK,' she answered hurriedly. 'He'll be fine. Now, I think you've done enough talking, Donny. They told me not to get . . . not to keep you talking for too long.'

'No. Tell me,' he insisted. 'Where is he? Is he all right?'

She hesitated. 'Donny, I'd prefer if we didn't talk about Liam now. I can understand that you're annoyed with him and I know he did some very foolish things, but just give him a chance to prove himself . . . .'

'Where is he?' Donny demanded.

'He's safe . . .'

'He's in jail, isn't he?'

'No, he's not!' she said, indignantly. 'He's here. In the Mater. They're letting him out today.'

'Here! You mean he's not hurt bad?'

'No. Well, except for two cracked ribs . . . but other than that . . . .'

'Well, you can tell him he'll have a few more cracked ribs if I have my way! Look at the mess he got me into! An' you too! Yeh, an' there's another thing. What about him hitting you the other day? We're not going to let him away with that, are we?'

'I know, Donny. But it won't happen again. He promised me.'

'Yeh!' Donny scoffed.

'Donny, please listen to me,' she was pleading with him now. 'I spoke to him again only this morning. He promised me on his solemn oath that he's going to try for that job with Caffreys' and keep out of trouble. Donny, he's sorry for hitting me. I know it! He was crying there in the bed only half an hour ago. He's not a bad oul' skin, Don. Just give him a chance.' Donny wasn't convinced, but he didn't want to be too hard on Maeve. He could see that she needed his support.

'But what about the cops, Maeve? Will they not be charging him?'

'I don't think so, Don. But that's what I wanted to talk to you about. We don't want you to tell any lies for Liam's sake, because he's already told them all about it. When they come this morning, just tell them what happened.'

'Yeh! But what did *he* tell them?' He tried to keep the cynicism out of his voice.

'He told them the truth. He was given the stuff to deliver, but he had second thoughts. He decided to go the Guards instead and that's when Slits and Dogs copped him. That's why he gave the stuff to you. He didn't think you'd get involved.' Donny listened, head down, his mind struggling between his mistrust of Liam and his loyalty to Maeve.

'Just give him a chance, Don,' she said quietly. He nodded.

'OK, Sis,' he said. 'One chance.'

'Thanks, Don.' When she kissed him on the cheek, her eyes were brimming with tears.

After Maeve left, Donny read the newspaper story to himself several times. He had to admit that it made good reading. It occurred to him, however, that he would probably be called to give evidence if Slits and his gang were brought to trial, and he knew that this would expose him to some danger. Slits and the others were not likely to forget the part that Donny had played in their capture, especially if they finished up in jail. Yet somehow, he was surprised to find that he was so unconcerned at the possibility of Slits' revenge — a possibility which, if he had become aware of it before Thursday last, would have had him weak at the knees with terror. He felt too that his life was changing — *had* changed even in the past few days. It wasn't all good, he knew. Down on the lake he had nearly been killed. Even in Cork Street and in the Park it was possible that a bullet could have got him. And where would he have been then? 'Dead,' he said aloud, 'bleedin' stone dead!' And there was still the problem at school. He was surprised that it didn't bother him more when he remembered. Ah, to hell with it, he thought. Even if I have to go down to Shaw Street, what about it? It won't be the end of the world.

He would miss Flagon and Swamp though. Yes, he told himself, he'd find it hard enough settling into a new school without the lads. The lads. Donny frowned. There was something different about them too. Maybe it was just the way he himself was on the previous evening, but he had a sense that they were seeing him in a different light. It was a good feeling, though. Somehow it was all part of the changes that were happening.

The best thing of all, however, was meeting Jacky. If someone had told him on Tuesday that by Friday he'd have gone through all that — on the boat — on the bike — in the Park — with a girl like Jacky, he'd have told them to get their head examined. It was just incredible — like a dream. 'Maybe it is a bleedin' dream,' he told himself. And suddenly he wanted to see Jacky. He wanted her to walk in through the curtains and sit on the bed and just *be* there — just be herself. He wondered where she was; where were the lads; where was everybody. He sat up in bed and listened. In the corridor outside the room, footsteps came and went. He focused his attention on every approaching sound, hoping that each set of footsteps would bring Jacky, or even Flagon or Swamp. But no-one came.

Donny was drifting into sleep when, a short time later, heavy footsteps thumped in through the doorway beside him. The nurse came through the curtains.

'You'd better sit up and take notice,' she said. 'There's two policemen here to see you.'

The big detective with the bushy moustache was accompanied by a young uniformed Garda who carried a narrow briefcase. When the introductions were done and the young Garda had been seated on the chair with a notepad and pen, the big detective said, 'Right, Donny. You can start at the beginning.'

Donny told them everything, pausing only when the big man interrupted occasionally to clarify a point or ask a question. When he had finished, the detective was silent for a moment while the Garda finished scribbling on his pad. Then he spoke.

'So that's how the stuff got into the car. That had us puzzled. It's not like that sort to leave illegal substances lying on the floor of their car. You realise, of course, that you could have come straight to the Gardaí when you first came into possession of that stuff.'

'Yes. I know, Guard,' Donny agreed. 'But, with everything happening, an' them havin' Maeve an' all . . .' The other nodded.

'We'll have to see if we can get the justice to take the circumstances into account.' The detective's face was serious and thoughtful. 'Not to mention the fact that you were in possession of two vehicles that didn't rightly belong to you.'

'I know, Guard,' Donny admitted, looking more contrite than ever. 'I just never thought about that. I just wanted to make sure my family was all right, an' that those pushers didn't get away after all they'd done.' He watched anxiously as the other thought about it. Finally the detective nodded.

'Uh huh. That's understandable, in the circumstances.' He stood up and the uniformed Garda followed suit. 'We'll probably be calling on you as a witness. You haven't any plans to leave the country in the near future?' he asked drily.

'You must be joking,' Donny quipped with a broad smile. 'Not unless there's a reward for lifting the gang an' the packet of stuff.'

The other shook his head ruefully. 'I'm afraid that only happens in books, sonny. But, if it's any consolation to you, the Commissioner thinks you did very well, and he'd like to have a chat with you sometime . . . and your girlfriend too, even if she did have her father worried sick, with her running off like that.' His face grew serious as he prepared to leave. 'You were both very lucky, you know. You could have been seriously injured or killed. That's why it's best to let the Gardaí handle situations like this.' It was all that Donny could do to restrain himself from exploding with indignation, but he held his fire. For Maeve's sake he wanted to stay on the right side of the authorities, at least until Liam was cleared. And so, the big detective nodded wisely down at him and went away contented.

When the police had left, the nurse brought Donny a cup of tea and more tablets. Then he settled down to wait for Jacky and the others to come. If they didn't come soon, he decided, he would sneak out of bed, find a telephone and call one of them. Then lulled by the hum of traffic in the street below, he dozed off.

14

'. . . You wouldn't think it, would you? I mean, to look at him there on the bed, you'd think he was a bit of a pansy . . .' Donny opened his eyes to see Jacky, Flagon, Swamp and Bill Moloney grinning down at him.

'Naw,' Swamp retorted. 'He's just waitin' for the pransome hincess to come along an' kiss him and wake him out of his beauty sleep. Mmmpuh!' Swamp's imitation of a princess's kiss left something to be desired. Donny grinned with pleasure.

'Hi, folks. Hi, Mr Moloney. How's things?'

Things appeared to be fine, for, in a moment or two, Flagon and Swamp were in full spate, and Donny could hardly get a word in edgeways.

'You shoulda see Magee's face when I hit him in the bread-bin with the loaf,' chortled Flagon. 'An' Don here was roarin' for me to do it again.' He shrugged his shoulders and spread his hands wide to the others. 'So what did I do?'

'Yeh,' said Swamp, his face deadpan. 'Went an' had a cuppa tea.'

'He musta been havin' a four-course dinner on the bonnet of the car, it took him so long to get stuck in, in the first place,' Donny joked.

'Ah, y'know what the coach says. Never do any strenuous exercise unless you're properly warmed up. Stretch the muscles, y'know.'

'Huh!' snorted Swamp. 'If we'd been thirty seconds later arrivin', you wouldn't have had any muscles left to stretch. The big ape in the car was just comin' to when we arrived. I can see it all now. There's Flag an' Don and Magee in a black knot on the ground, an' Flag's roarin', "We got him, Don! We got him!" An' suddenly this huge black shadow starts to creep up along the back of his neck!'

'No sweat!' retorted Flagon, and then the slagging began in earnest. Donny left them at it, hammer and tongs. He stole a glance at Jacky. She wore a light blue sweatshirt and white canvas trousers, and her blonde hair was swept back and held loosely by a blue ribbon behind. He wanted to say something brilliant or funny but his mind seemed to go blank all of a sudden. In panic he patted the bed beside him with his hand and opened his mouth. A sound emerged which, as he later wryly observed, sounded like the mating call of the duckbilled platypus. He cleared his throat and tried again.

'Sit down,' he managed. She sat. Her eyes were bright.

'How's things?' she asked.

He cleared his throat again. 'Fine . . . good . . . great, in fact.' Jeez! he said to himself. Get a hold of yourself. Bill Moloney intervened.

'Sleep OK, Donny?'

'Ah, yeh. Fine . . . great,' Donny said. 'How's Moira?' He had always said 'Mrs Moloney' before.

'She's nearly recovered, Donny.' Bill replied. 'A good night's sleep works wonders. When I left, she was getting ready to bake one of her specialties. We think a little celebration is in order.' There was a knowing twinkle in his eye.

'Yeh,' said Donny ruefully. 'I missed out on the porter cake the other night.'

'Well, we'd like you and the lads and Maeve and Jacky to come up as soon as you're on your feet again. It's the least we can do to thank you for getting us out of a pretty awkward situation.'

'I'm sorry I got you an' Moira into it in the first place.'

'Don't worry about it, Donny.' Bill paused for a moment, looking steadily at Donny. 'I had a chat with Brother O'Connor last night.'

'Oh, yeh?' Donny was suddenly interested. Jacky, Flagon and Swamp were listening with obvious anticipation.

'He spoke to Brother Sharkey, after he heard about your . . . escapade. There's no need to go into the gory details, but let us just say that Brother Sharkey is prepared to see your little, eh, disagreement in a different light, having taken account of the domestic pressures which you were under the other day.'

'You serious?' Donny was scarcely able to believe what he had just heard.

'Yes,' Bill went on. 'He's prepared to recommend your return to the school, on probation, mind you.'

'Probation?' Donny's ardour was slightly dampened. 'Who? Me or him?'

The others were looking uneasily at Bill Moloney.

'Look, Donny,' Bill opened his hands in a gesture of entreaty. 'We have to let him think that he's in control, that he's saved face. Probation is only a form of words. It doesn't really mean anything because, knowing you, there isn't going to be any more trouble anyway.'

Donny thought about it. Out of the corner of his eye he caught Flagon's apprehensive glance in Swamp's direction. Getting back to school, he thought, couldn't be as easy as this.

'All right,' he demanded. 'What's the catch?'

Bill looked for support. Flagon was gazing pointedly out through the window; Swamp was busily examining his hands. Jacky looked expectantly at Bill and Bill took a deep breath.

'They want a letter,' he said evenly. Donny's hackles rose. 'A letter! From who?'

'From you, Donny. Look, it's just a formality.'

'You mean apologise, an' lick up to them?'

'Ah, come on, Don,' Flagon broke in. 'Only a few sentences. Just to get back to the old kip. You don't have to mean it.'

'No way!' Donny cut him short. 'There's no way I'll write that letter. Not to him! He's the one who should be apologising. He nearly laid me out with a punch!'

Flagon studied Donny's face for a minute. Then he turned and nodded decisively towards Swamp.

'Wise decision, Don,' said Swamp, his words dripping with understanding. 'Wouldn't bother with a letter if I was you.' He reached into the inside pocket of his jacket and extracted a clean, white envelope, which he held aloft in his pudgy fingers. Donny saw that it was addressed to, 'Revd Brother Sharkey'. 'Y'see,' continued Swamp. 'It's already written.' A sardonic smile played around the corners of his mouth. Donny stared in disbelief. Flagon pushed home the advantage.

'C'mon, Don,' he argued. 'We can't let you off down to St Kierans or one of them other schools where all they probably know about you is that you did a McGyver on Slits an' Dogs. You wouldn't be there three days till you'd have a huge swelled head. Y'see, you *need* us an' the lads, Don. We *know* you. *We're* the only ones that can keep you from gettin' too big for your boots. Just think, Don. We'll be doin' you a big favour if we send this letter to Jaws. Now, come on. Be a sensible lad an' sign it.' Donny was beginning to sense how much each of them wanted him to come back to the school. He felt himself weakening, but he wasn't going to give them an easy victory.

'You don't think I'm going to sign something when I haven't even seen what's written on it?' Flagon turned triumphantly to Swamp. 'Read it, son,' he commanded.

Swamp solemnly took the letter from the envelope, opened it, cleared his throat dramatically, stepped back one pace to take him out of Donny's reach, and began.

'Dear Jaws, Sorry I hadn't me spear-gun an' me flippers on me the other morn . . .'

Flagon nearly blew his top. 'Ah, come on!' he hissed through gritted teeth. 'The real one, Swamp!' Swamp, pretending surprise, looked out at them over his glasses.

'Oh, the real one, is it?' Jacky, who had been trying to keep a serious face, gave up the struggle and laughed outright. Flagon made a drive at Swamp and whipped the letter out of his hand.

'Don't mind him,' said Flagon. 'He's not in possession of his faculties this morning. This is how the letter goes.' He composed himself, and then read.

'Dear Brother Sharkey, I refer to the incident in which I was involved in the MD room on the morning of last Thursday. I wish you to know that I regret the trouble that it has caused. I will do my best to ensure that such an incident will not happen again.' He lowered the letter and watched Donny expectantly. Donny left them dangling a little longer.

'Who wrote that load of boloney?' he asked. The tension was broken. Bill smiled in recognition of his personal catch-word. 'We all did, Don,' he said. 'We are certain that it expresses nothing but the truth.'

'Yeh, well, that depends on Jaws, and how he carries on,' retorted Donny.

They let him have the last word. Jacky was wriggling a pen significantly between her fingers. Donny leaned forward and reached for it.

'OK, I'm only doing this for you lot,' he told them, as he signed the letter.

Soon afterwards, the doctor arrived to examine Donny. A tall, dark-haired woman, she seemed genuinely interested in Donny's story. Flagon and Swamp, who hadn't politely withdrawn with Bill and Jacky, gave her the full blow-by-blow description. Donny marvelled at their genuine powers of narration: the slight exaggeration here, the slight fiction there, that made the whole escapade seem like a TV thriller.

'I can see that your friends are anxious to have you out, young man,' the doctor remarked after she had examined the wound on Donny's thigh. 'But I'd like you to stay for a little while longer. Probably until tomorrow. We must let that wound heal a little more before we let you into circulation again. It needs rest, and I have a suspicion that you won't get much of that if I release you to these eager beavers.' She winked at Donny as she rose to go.

When the doctor had gone, Bill Moloney came back through the curtains.

'So, you're here until tomorrow, eh? In that case I'll head off for a while and come back later this evening. Either of you two lads want a lift back to base?'

'Eh, no thanks,' Flagon began. Then suddenly he seemed to change his mind. Donny could have sworn he saw Swamp kick Flagon on the ankle. 'Then, on the other hand, it's a long walk over. We might as well take the lift.' Swamp tugged at Flagon's elbow and they both moved towards the curtain.

'After all,' said Swamp, 'a fella needs a bit of privacy now and again.' He threw an exaggerated wink in Donny's direction and left. From outside the curtain came Swamp's voice again. 'Go easy on the TLC now, Jacky,' and then the boys were gone.

When Jacky appeared once again through the curtains, Donny thought that her cheeks seemed a little more flushed that usual. To tell the truth, he wasn't feeling too cool himself.

'Hi,' she called.

'Hi,' he croaked, aware that his own face was beginning to burn. She stood close to the bed and he noticed the blue shadow on her left cheek where Slits had hit her.

'Sit down — if you like,' he said lamely, pulling the hospital pyjamas more tightly around him, so that they wouldn't look quite so much like a sack. He knew his hair was all over the place and that his face was probably covered with colourful bruises. Jacky sat on the bed beside him. Looking at her face and neck, Donny was acutely aware of her closeness. Through his mind, for a split second, flashed the idea that he was in the presence of a total stranger. Say something, you dummy you, his mind told him.

'Well, what did she say?' Jacky asked, smiling.

'Who?'

'Who d'you think? The doctor, of course.'

'Oh, yeh. Nothin' much. I mean I can't remember.' Jacky's eyebrows went up. 'I mean, she said I was OK and that I'd be out of here tomorrow.'

She studied him intently for a moment. 'Are you OK?' Her smile reassured him.

'Yeh,' he said, 'it must be the drugs they're feedin' me here. Anyway, thanks for comin' in to see me.'

'I had it all planned to come earlier, and then so many things happened. First of all, the Guards rang to say they wanted to talk to me again.' She waved a dismissive hand. 'Oh, just the same stuff as yesterday. And then . . .' She nudged him in delight. 'Mum rang — from England. Guess what? She's coming home!' The warmth of her happiness washed over him. 'Y'see, Dad rang her when he realised I was gone, thinking that maybe we'd gone to England, and she's been in touch several times since. I had a really long chat with her and I told her about you and what happened on the lake. Anyway, she's coming home. Isn't it great!' Impulsively, she grabbed his hand. 'I think they're going to try to make it up.' In the corner of her eye he saw a tear forming.

'Oh, that's cool, Jacky. But what about Veronica?' he blurted out.

'She's gone,' she answered, managing a smile. 'Dad said she had a delicate stomach and wasn't used to water, but I think she began to lose interest after I ran away. That gave her a fright. And I don't think she was too happy about being bundled back to Dublin at short notice.'

'Ah, the woodworm,' Donny quipped. 'That's what did it.' She couldn't help but laugh.

'Well, her opinion of me went downhill fast when she found out I'd run off with a criminal — a drug-pusher and joy-rider and God knows what else!' she retorted.

'Yeh, you can't trust that sort,' Donny agreed sternly, happy that she was laughing. 'A bad lot. They'd take advantage of you like a shot, they would.'

'You're beginning to sound just like my dad. That's exactly what he thought till he read that bit about us in the paper. Now he's dying to meet you.'

'Oh, sure. That's one meeting I'm going to make sure to miss. I know dads and their precious little daughters.'

'No, honest,' she insisted, tugging at his hand. 'He wants to meet you. He really does. I've told him all about you. Don't say you're going to back out on me now!' He knew then that it was important to her.

'OK, if you really want me to, I will.'

'Thanks,' she said simply. She looked down at his hand firmly holding hers and was silent for a moment. 'Oh, Donny, I'm so happy.' A tear trickled down her cheek. Then Donny surprised himself. 'C'mere,' he said, and leaning forward, he put his arms around her. She leaned against him and nestled her head against his shoulder. He felt the soft rhythm of her sobbing through her cotton sweatshirt.

'Things sometimes turn out better than you expect them,' he said. Her head nodded up and down on his shoulder.

'Donny,' she whispered, after what seemed a long time, 'you'll have to let me go.' He tightened his grip around her slim body. 'What's the magic word?' he asked.

'The magic word is that Daddy's been waiting outside the door for the past half hour.'

'You're kidding. That old trick won't work.'

'I'm not, Donny,' she said, and her body shook with laughter.

'Oh, yes, you are,' he said in his best panto style. 'You're only trying to scare me.'

'Oh, no, I'm not. Do you want me to prove it?'

'Go ahead,' he challenged.

'Daddy,' she sang out.

He heard the heavy footsteps first. When Jacky's dad walked in through the curtains, Jacky was sitting on the bedside chair, bent over with laughter.

'Great sufferin' duck!' said Donny aloud.

ACE fiction

Look out for more great fiction from Wolfhound Press!

Judith and the Traveller

Mike Scott

Judith Meredith is on the run.

Life has been tough since her mother died, but on the day her wealthy father remarries the answer seems simple. All she has to do is leave....

But she does not know Dublin. And when three toughs get nasty, Judith realises she lacks street wisdom.

Luckily, Spider turns up. Judith has never known anybody like him — a young traveller living on the roadside, and a good friend....

Staying together isn't easy — but the longer she spends with Spider, the more Judith likes him.

And what of tomorrow?

Being pursued by parents, police and travellers, the teenagers realise their days together are numbered — but they are not going to give in without a fight....

£3.99 Paperback
Another great ACE story from Wolfhound

BOOK NEWS

Would you like to get the lastest news on new, exciting books as they are published? Just fill in the coupon and send it to us at Wolfhound Press, 68 Mountjoy Square, Dublin 1.

On Borrowed Ground

Hugh FitzGerald Ryan
£4.99 Paperback £10.95 Hardback

A tale of wry humour, of cynicism and of hope, a tale reminiscent of days that are gone, yet whose vividly-painted characters remain with us long after the last page is turned.

The Voyage of Mael Duin

Patricia Aakhus McDowell
£11.95 Hardback

A dramatic Celtic novel. Mael Duin, the child of a fierce warrior and young nun, is raised as a chieftain's heir. At the age of sixteen he discovers his true parentage, sets off on the western sea to avenge his father, and a saga unfolds....

Please send me news of Wolfhound Press books.

Name _____

Address_____

All prices are correct at time of going to print.

Liam O'Flaherty

A master weaver of words

Mr Gilhooley
£4.99 Paperback

A brilliant thriller of the Dublin underworld. Described by
W.B. Yeats as 'a great novel', on publication, it was as famous
as James Joyce's *Ulysses*.

Famine
£5.95 Paperback

"A major achievement – a masterpiece .... it is the kind of
truth only a major writer of fiction is capable of portraying"
— Anthony Burgess

Skerrett
£3.95 Paperback

"Yes, O'Flaherty left bruises and sore bones behind him but
he could also, as he still can, shake the house with laughter
... this tragic novel ... this remarkable book ... *Skerrett* is a
classic" — *Irish Times*